SOUR HONEY

Mary Abago

Fountain Publishers

Fountain Publishers Ltd
P.O. Box 488
Kampala,
Uganda

ISBN 9970 02 147 8

CHAPTER ONE

I sometimes imagine there will be a time when God will be tired of controlling all his property and he will decide to put them under the control of man. But the confusion that will reign at that time I cannot yet imagine. Hitler would sell off his dear mother and dear wife for hell so that he could bake all the Jews and poor blacks in it. Terrorists would struggle for the governors of hell so that the whole world would be sent shaking. Musicians would steal God's angels before he declares the right heirs. Napoleon would head straight for God's throne, and no one would stop him from doing that ,so that he can have the whole world in his palms. But I know what I would remain for I would gather people from all walks of life, failures and heroes, tycoons and paupers, women and men and lead a very great procession to God. We would never ask for anything great. We would only want to know why, how, and sincerely why? We would only want to know. Why does he allow some things to happen? How does he make them happen? But is he the one behind such happenings? If he is not the one behind such disasters, why does he give malicious hands responsibility? Why does he choose this man not the other one to be a pauper? What is the method for choosing people to be what they are? Is God not biased when dealing with his children? We would want to know. Should we blame God, should we blame someone else, or should we blame us? We would want to know and we would never ask for anything again. We would never disturb God again; perhaps we would be satisfied.

She was Maria. The most learned being in her village. She was an example for everyone. She was talked about everywhere in the village.

"The world is really changing," they would say, "even women nowadays are equally able."

"See Maria. She has read books and books."

"We wish all our daughters could be like that."

"But Maria alone is enough to show those men that we can also be like them," the woman would say, "and soon we shall catch up with them."

Everyone agreed that Maria was beautiful, Maria was a brilliant learned girl, and so the talk went on.

* * *

Simeon was quite a famous man. He was old and had wisdom in him. This made him revered throughout the village.

Now he was sitting on a stool near the fire. He was feeling a bit of fatigue after hunting. His head was raised and he was absent-mindedly admiring the stars. The fire was over-heating his legs and he kept on rubbing them. This made him appear half bent. Around the fire were his grandchildren and daughter – his last born. She also called him grandfather. In fact, she felt more of a grandchild than a daughter. This could have been due to the fact that by the time she was born, Simeon already had grown-up grandchildren who assimilated her into their ways. Simeon loved his daughter só much that his love for his wife was dwindling. His love was Stella.

It was Stella who brought back Simeon's mind from counting the stars. "I wish I was like Maria," she started. "Very beautiful and very good at books. At times, I feel God lacks the sense of proportion. He gives too much to some and to others too little or nothing at worst. If he was to give to all equally, there would be no worrying." She ended her speech with a sneer.

"Stella, stop blaming God," he rebuked her in a sharp tone. Simeon had great fear of God and he believed that any such thing would bring disaster, which he feared more than God himself. But when he talked again, his tone had gone back to normal. "I don't think it's God who does that. I always believe that God leaves it to man to decide a great percentage of the way he should live his life. The problem is that few people have discovered this. I don't think it's God who made Maria great and you simple. She chose to work and you chose to be lazy. Maria has got the spirits of her father. Oweka is a man who is stern, tireless and determined to fight to the bitter end. I saw him from his childhood to now..."

"No! Grandfather, I don't believe you, you are lying. Are you trying to tell me that Maria worked hard to become beautiful?"

"No child..."

"Yes, that's what I meant. She was born beautiful, what did she do?"

"No child," Simeon insisted, "let me tell you the truth and you'll learn. We don't need to blame God every time we fail. And we should not thank him every time we succeed, Stella!

2

"Yes, we should always examine what has caused what and thank or blame it. Whether God or man.

"I saw Oweka from his childhood," he began without ceremony, "and I know what he has passed through to become what he is now."

So Simeon began his story.

Oweka was the son of a man who was a total failure, a drunk and a domestic warlord. He kept on beating his wife whenever he felt like. If all men were like that then I would have prayed to God to create a third sex. Perhaps that sex would be considerate to women. It was hard to see the reasons why he called himself the father of the family. Oweka's mother did all the work. She alone did the digging, she alone built houses, granaries and whenever Oweka's father was angry, he quenched his anger upon her. If it was for love of Oweka's father, she would have long left him but for the sake of her children she endured. Hers was a donkey's task, she was walking bones with the expression of sadness all over her.

At the age of thirteen, Oweka could understand. He gave some help to his mother. All of us were happy, we knew Oweka would relieve his mother soon. All suffering women look to their children as a relief in the long run. Oweka showed this at a tender age.

Then one day, Oweka stayed at home cooking, while his mother went digging. Usually, his mother came back after a while to supervise him, but that day she didn't. Oweka did everything hurriedly and felt a need to find out why his mother had not come back. He decided to go and relieve her. From a distance, he could hear the baby crying. Several questions started flocking into his mind. Is the child sick? Could be Mama has decided to run to their home? Maybe she is sick... He decided to run, he wanted to find out what was wrong. His heart drummed with fear. He wanted to know and yet he feared to know. He reached the scene and what he saw, he tried to convince himself was unreal. It was hard to believe and yet it was hard truth. His head turned round and round and round, he was dizzy with faint reasoning, he cursed the night and the bed where he was conceived.

On the ground, lay his mother, on her stomach. The baby on her back tied with a dirty piece of cloth struggled in vain to free itself. In her right hand was a hoe. The sun stood at the centre of the earth, the heat was too great and the ground was steaming. Grasshoppers sang in disagreement with the heat and seemed to mock Oweka. In all directions stretched the

3

plain, brown decorated with trees here and there. Even with the heat, people were still busy in the fields. For how long had she been dead? Oweka called for help among the people working in their fields. They gathered and carried the dead body home. Oweka followed them from behind, carrying the child and too desperate at heart. The message soon spread throughout the village and the neighbourhood. Men came quietly, expressing their emotions, women came wailing as though it was the first time they had known death, but the most affected people were the relatives of the dead woman, and mostly her mother. A trace of tears could not be seen anywhere but she was sadness everywhere. She talked this and talked that and everyone understood that she was blaming Oweka's father for her daughter's death. People mourned for her but to be frank I did not. I knew from deep inside me that she had got her freedom. She died labouring and it was this burden that rested her. My tears were for the children. The elder son only thirteen years old, with an irresponsible father – what would become of them?

That day, Oweka's father came back home late in the night. He was singing merrily, mouthing his wife's name at intervals and demanding food. On hearing this, his mother-in-law almost went crazy. She started wailing, the tone carrying sad memories. Oweka's father was taken aback but he soon grasped the atmosphere at his home. There were very many people sitting sadly and a fire lit at the centre of his courtyard.

"What is wrong?" he asked nervously. But everyone kept quiet. He asked the second time and again did not get a reply. He felt sober and knew that his presence was hated. He stepped inside and found more shock when he saw a group of women seated with their chins in their palms, around one that was lying. He knew it all instantly.

"Who is dead?" he asked. He received answers that made his heart sink. His mother-in-law attacked him bitterly.

"There is your meat, you can eat it. Boil her, eat her, you wicked man, you killed my daughter. Yes, you killed her... you made her work... like ... like a donkey and now she is ... she is de..e..ad... eat her please, cook her..."

He wanted to reply but this was no time for explanation. He knew everyone around was against him. No one would support him if anyone was to rise against him. He decided to escape from all the blame and glaring eyes by proceeding to his room, his heart so heavy. He rested his

4

thin self on the papyrus bed. It was very chilly but he did not care. Previously, he would have first rubbed the papyrus to make it warm, but today he just fell on it, he did not realise the cold. Inside him, he was wondering and questioning, "So my wife is dead? So they are blaming me? But am I really to blame?" He soon fell asleep before he could worry a lot.

At his wife's burial, everyone was puzzled to see that Oweka's father shed tears. Some of the people thought that he cried because at long last he had realised his mistake. It made him understand that he had always been in the wrong. It was a sign of repentance, a kind of sorry to his wife, getting reconciled to her before she was taken deep down. But most people believed that his tears were because of fear. He was fearing responsibility. Who would do all that his wife used to do? His donkey was dead! Some people did not care and they mocked at him.

Oweka's father became a very sad man. He did not drink, he did not leave his home, he was always by the side of his children. He had learnt a lesson, we all agreed. Everything has got a good side to it. We were so depressed about Oweka's mother's death but thought that it taught his father how to be responsible.

We were however mistaken. The effect of his wife's death was only shortlived. A month after the sad moments, he resumed his previous life. He went back to drinking he quarrelled and beat his children. Oweka took the place of his mother. Every night, his father surveyed his buttocks with strokes of the cane.

He felt hatred for his father and in his mind, he was determined to end his life. He prayed for his father's death and wished that his father had died and his mother lived. He was very young, his father beat him and yet he had to work for his brothers' living. He could not endure any more so he decided to run to his aunt. But this was no solution. His father discovered him and he was got back immediately with severe punishment. He threatened a very serious punishment to anyone who would harbour Oweka in his home. This frightened everyone and no one could help Oweka for fear of danger.

Oweka could not provide for the children as his mother had done. They were falling sick frequently, they became under nourished and were more or less naked. The youngest child his mother had left behind was the first to die. Five months later an epidemic broke out in the land. It

5

wasn't very serious but because of lack of a cure his other two brothers died a week after each other. Oweka's father became so desperate. No one could say he was pretending, nor could we say he had not yet learnt. He realised his helplessness , he realised how his life was dying away bit by bit. He tried to reform but it was impossible. His troubles could not allow him to live with a clear head. He wanted a place to hide from reality. No place apart from alcohol was around. He drank with the only hope of following his family one day. He drank and he did not eat. Soon he started developing swellings. His death was easy. At his dying moment, he asked Oweka to forgive him. No one knows whether Oweka did.

During his mother's lifetime and after her death, Oweka had always felt angry with his father. He had hoped to pay for his mother's suffering. But now with everybody gone he felt sad. He realised that even his father's useless presence was important. The world became different. It was as if it were doomsday. It is at times better to feel angry rather than sad. An angry man can move mountains with his anger but a sad man is worse than a completely crippled child. He lacks the energy, the zeal and the will to do. Oweka was ever worried, ever crying. Whenever you greeted him he replied with tears. You would not look at him twice.

In this land, people love you for what you are, not who you are. Oweka became an alien in the society. No one loved him. People chased him from their homes. He did not even eat what was given to the dogs. Even his true relatives ignored him. He tried working for a living in people's homes. But this too was sad. In most cases, when he worked he was sent away empty-handed. On rare occasions he was given only food that dogs would themselves not eat. After all he had no voice strong enough to talk, neither had he the backing of relatives. It became worse when he got jiggers all over his body and he could not walk very well. The only hut his people had left for him collapsed. Disaster does not strike once. It comes in chains. The world seemed nothing to Oweka. He also started to long for his death but, unlike his father whose wish was fulfilled, Oweka did not die. What could he do with his life? He wanted a solution to his problems. He prayed night and day. At night he prayed with the hope that he would wake up in the morning to find a miracle had happened. In the day time he would pray and keep watch until midnight. He took his only hen and went to my friend the soothsayer for counselling.

After receiving the hen, the soothsayer observed Oweka all over and sighed. His eyes, one could see, depicted a heavy task ahead. He signed again. Oweka almost cried. He concluded that the good in life was not his, but he still remained patient. The man picked a stone from one of his pots; it was shiny and it showed that it had been used for ages. He handed it over to Oweka.

"Here," he said. "Whisper all your problems to that stone and give it back." Oweka put the stone close to his mouth and his lips started moving. Whatever things he mentioned no one knows. No one could hear him. The soothsayer got back the stone and put it close to his ear. He remained quiet for sometime and then suddenly began to whistle. His face relaxed, Oweka's heart relaxed too.

"My child," the soothsayer started his prophecy, "Things seem not to be so bad for you. Nonetheless there is a great mountain between you and your fortune. You might not move it if you don't spend energy."

"What then should I have to do?" Oweka asked in a bothered tone. The soothsayer straightened his back and started encouraging Oweka, "Immediately you dislodge this mountain, I can see, yes I can see it now, child, that you will have pots of happiness. The only thing you have to do is to chase the wind!"

Oweka was puzzled by this. "What do you mean by chasing the wind?"

"I don't have to spoonfeed you, boy. Go now and begin your race, chase the wind, catch it, and you'll have succeeded."

Oweka left in total confusion. How was he going to chase the wind? That was the trick of soothsayers, they always told you the impossible. "He knew of course that I cannot catch the wind however much I run," Oweka thought. "Then he will have to blame me for being lazy. Why did I go to the bastard soothsayer?" Oweka regretted." He is too stupid to know that wind cannot be chased. How can one chase wind?" he kept on asking himself but he could not find an answer. Besides this, Oweka had had enough of his jiggers and knew that running after the wind would mean borrowing someone else's legs. Oweka felt hated, more lonely and a complete alien in his own society. He felt the soothsayer with low spirits, disgusted with the world, and felt he would have been happy if he had been dead. He reached his compound. There was nothing left for him apart from the graves and the bare compound.

He tuned round and looked in the four directions. He saw no sign of mercy and love. He took the last decision. He left the land, following a narrow footpath, and disappeared through the forests. Before this he had thought a native could not become an alien. He became one, so he left.

We saw him leave and we wondered what was wrong but we knew he would come back. It was merely the act of a desperate man. He was only being a fool, after all he had no kin who was willing to take up responsibility. No one wanted more burdens. He would wander from home to home and after a day or two, he would come back. We waited. A day passed, two days, a week, a month, a year and Oweka was nowhere to be seen. Each day gave us the hope that he would come back tomorrow. Tomorrow came but Oweka never came. What had gone wrong? We waited but no one came. We concluded he was dead. Maybe he committed suicide, we thought. Perhaps some animal killed him. Maybe he died in the forest. He could have starved to death.

Five years after his departure, we all agreed that Oweka was dead. Various people came with varying stories and the rest combined the stories to create one big story that convinced us that Oweka was dead. It was only unfortunate that Oweka had no caring relatives, otherwise, a last funeral rite would have been done in his honour.

A problem arose in the village. People started claiming Oweka's land. Everyone had a reason for ownership. A group came and claimed that they were the right people to take the land because they were close family friends to Oweka's family. Some said they were the immediate neighbours to Oweka's family. They could not therefore see the reason why distant people came to claim the land on the mere fact of being family friends. Others said they were Oweka's relatives and they were the rightful people to take care of the property of their dead. If Oweka had been there at that time, I am sure he would have been the happiest man on earth. After a long period of loneliness, Oweka at last had people who wanted responsibility over him. To discover he had friends, neighbours and relatives would have been great.

At the end of the same year, Oweka came back! Through the same footpath. What mystery! What was behind it all? We started looking round for people who had said that Oweka was dead. But was it Oweka? It was his ghost perhaps. But he lived among us, he talked and ate. It was not a ghost. It was Oweka. He had come back. A full grown man. He had money, he was handsome and had shoes instead of jiggers. Everyone gaped in wonderment. What was the mystery? But where had he gone? What had he done there? What did he get there? It was a true mystery. In my mind I realised that Oweka had indeed set out to chase the wind but he had not known it. I felt like reminding him but I kept quiet because some people hate going back into their past.

Yes, when Oweka came back, he found people about to take up arms over his land. Oweka did not do anything about it but of course we knew that if he had found a man settled on his land, he would have woken up in the morning to find his head missing! Despite the fact that Oweka was very serious, we laughed over his statement. A head missing from the supreme body obviously means a dead body. How then does a dead man wake up to see himself dead? We laughed.

The very people who were struggling for Oweka's land were the first to become Oweka's friends. All of them had the message to convey, "You see, so-and-so wanted to take up your land, claiming he had a relationship with you but I scared him off. I even told him that the child Oweka might come back in need of it, so you leave it. You see people here are fools, I wonder how they came to conclude that you were dead. In fact they were about to organise the last funeral rite for you and yet you are here, as strong as a horse. Ha-ha-ha-ha-ha." They ended up accusing one another. Oweka got the full story but he merely kept quiet. He did not tell anyone where he had gone. He simply told us: "I have struggled and suffered."

We started gathering myths again and decided that Oweka had been to a big town where he worked for some rich man. After getting enough to start him off, he came back to the land of his ancestors, to his land and that of his descendants. He came back with ready muscles to work and he set to work. He built a hut for himself and started clearing thickets. The forest area became plots. He laboured like a donkey, he worked from morning to sunset and at times went beyond human tolerance. We admired his energy and we talked of him. But he kept aloof from us. He only greeted us and went back to hoeing. His only companion was his songs. He sang of his people: those he saw and those who died before he could see them. He sang about himself, about why people love you and many other songs we could not understand.

The next year, most people tried Oweka's way. But it's true when people say that the way that will lead me to heaven may not be the one that will lead you there too. People disappeared from the village one by one. You didn't see them leave but you discovered they had left days after their departure. They went to big towns. The very same people started coming back stealthily. They had failed and they came back in shame. The very lucky ones came back with the same status but those whose fates had worked against them came back in tatters. It was a year of shame, we remarked.

Oweka had his ambition with a vision. He worked and he achieved. He was never fruitless. The gods have rewarded him in all ways. They have never envied him because he prayed and worked, he was poor but had ambition. He is now a great man but what has he passed through to become great? Stop blaming God. Work with a heart and you'll get what you want. You can see what Oweka has passed through to become what he is now.

Simeon concluded. He turned round expecting to find the children gaping and convinced that people should blame themselves not God but was disappointed to find that everybody apart from Stella was asleep. He was disappointed. He did not however realise that his Oweka "Things" were too long. He kept quiet and did not show his disappointment. He waited for a comment from Stella but she did not talk. He felt uneasy. It seemed to him that all along no one was paying attention to him. He tried to cut the lull.

"Stella, that's how the world can be for some people."

"Grandfather, were you there during all that time all these things were happening?'

"I thought I told you in the beginning that I observed Oweka from his childhood to now."

"Then you are also not a good man."

"Why?"

"You also love people for what they are not for who they are. Why could you not give Oweka shelter, why could you not give him food, water? You could have taken him as your son, you could have been his relative though not exactly true. Why could you not do all these and yet you talk as though you were not among the people who denied Oweka a living?"

10

"I don't know, I really don't know. At times I think I am also bad but I think I am not very bad. I think it was fate working. If I had helped Oweka he would have felt at home and he would not have gone to fetch greatness."

"Then you should not blame others too, because if they had given Oweka food, he would not have gone."

"Yes, you are right." Simeon knew what Stella was driving him to. He had to stop the argument by agreeing with her. His head was working out how to change the topic. He found it. "You see my girl," he started, "There was a time when some white man came to this village. His aim was to put up a school for the black monkeys. He called us black monkeys. Whenever he tried to put up a building, he would wake up the next morning to find out that some hands had reduced the work to the initial stage. He did not give up. He told us that all would be well. 'It is known that a bad beginning makes a good ending and a good beginning makes a bad ending,' he said. He kept on hoping for a good ending and it indeed came true. All our learned boys are a result of his persistence. Oweka had it bad in the beginning, but with persistence, he has had a fine ending."

"But Oweka has not yet come to an end."

"He is now a big man. What else does he have to work for?"

"Grandfather, is it true that a good beginning makes a bad end and a bad beginning makes a good end?"

"Yes, sometimes, but of course you don't have to relax because you are a poor child and you think things will stay that way. Even rich children, when they work hard will remain great."

"That means that Oweka's children will have a bad end because they are now having a good beginning?"

"Stella, but I told you it depends upon how you work."

"No grandfather, this is the saying 'A good beginning, a bad end, a bad beginning, a good end.' Isn't it?"

"Stella, you ask very many questions. Take the children to sleep." He picked up his stool and left. He had lost his patience with Stella. She was fond of arguments. Simeon was disturbed by his daughter's comments. He loved Maria so much and he never wanted her to have a bad end. For him, Maria was unique. He thought she was the only

11

learned woman on earth. He imagined a time when Maria would die, imagined the whole world mourning. What Simeon had not known was that in every place there was a Maria. Perhaps two or more, even greater. His ignorance kept him so close to Maria that he almost worshipped her. He loved her, he wanted her to live.

CHAPTER TWO

How Oweka lived a happy life is one of the wonders of the village. A stranger cannot easily believe Oweka's past. It's true people can suffer. It's also true Oweka should be pitied. But where does the pity go now? Oweka lived a full, happy life, the richest man in the village. His problem was not money. His problem was how to use money. But Oweka was not happy with his property alone, he had the pride of having an exemplary daughter. The most learned girl Maria, his only daughter, was the pillar of his pride. Her full names were Adirisa Maria. Her first name carries a story.

After Oweka came back from his treasure land, he set to work and after accumulating enough wealth, he decided to get married. He picked a woman from a distant village. This was bad news for the local girls. All of them had expected Oweka to choose from among them, with each one thinking she would be the choice. Oweka knew this but he took no notice and he disappointed all of them. For was it not they and their parents who threw him away? This woman however, did not live up to Oweka's expectations. In the village a woman's value was weighed by the number of children she produced. No one believed that it could be the man's fault. Barren women were beaten as though it was their choice to be barren. But this was not the case with Maria's mother. She bore many children but all of them joined the dead at a tender age. This was disaster for Oweka. People chided him for "picking" a foreign woman. "How can you pick a woman when you don't know her origin?" they said. Foreign blood was never a blessing. There was no way Oweka could be regarded as a man in the society. After all he ploughed gardens and they never yielded what could be eaten.

Oweka's wife was despised. She had no value. What was a woman who had no child? Every man mocked her. Oweka regretted marrying from a distant place. He came to hate his wife and he felt a need to send her away.

There is a belief in that village that if a woman's children keep on dying, then there is a jealous evil spirit that kills them. The evil spirit is believed to be from the woman's clan. The woman will therefore be returned to her family so that her clan members can cleanse her. Oweka did this, too. He was desperate for a child. This would be his last

13

endeavour. If it failed, then he would find another woman who could please him.

By the time Oweka took his wife back to her family, she was seven months heavy. He harassed her people and told them he would divorce their daughter there and then if the situation could not be altered. "I married your daughter so that she can give me offspring. I don't want graves, I want children. What is she doing for me? What is her work in my home? How could you give me such a wife? You knew she was dirty and you made me pay the price. I am giving her the last chance. If her next child dies, then you take her back and I will need my cows!" His mother-in-law tried to plead with him, explained that it wasn't her choice. She begged him to be patient, saying nothing could be done until the time she would be giving birth and after. She convinced Oweka that everything would be fine, that would work over it and they would get a blessing of children. Oweka left without another word and went back home alone. His mother in law had reassured him.

He was however, desperate at heart. What if things did not happen in the way he wanted? What else would he do? He started developing a need for a second wife. What was a man without a child? A child is the true happiness of a man. Animals, crops, money are nothing. A child is wealth. Oweka felt like starting a search for a woman. He saw time running against him. He was getting on in years yet he had no child. At his age, he should have a son of ten. In his heart there was an urge to find another woman as soon as he could. But still he was ready to be patient.

Oweka started ticking days away. He knew she was already seven months heavy. She therefore had two more months but, for fear of tension, he added one more month. He counted and counted but days whirled round him and did not move away. Hours tripled. He kept on looking towards the road leading to his wife's home expecting good news but nothing came.

At long last, his wife's brother came. He was excited when he talked to Oweka. The woman had given birth to a baby girl. A cleansing ceremony was to be done two days afterwards and Oweka was wanted immediately. His presence was very important.

When Oweka arrived the ceremony started. One man was sent to Oweka's home to get it ready for visitors. He had some duties to do there. His work was to cleanse the home.

14

Oweka and his wife were stripped naked, the child was wrapped in a barkcloth and they were left in that state for the two days before the real ceremony. They were not to leave the room. They ate and went for calls in the same room. They were not to talk to each other or to anyone else. After the two days, a gap, a bit larger than a normal window, was made through the wall of the house where the parents and child were. The mother and child were passed through this gap. This means that the evil spirit that kills children and that waits for them in the doorway would get tired and go to the forest. Mother and child were then taken to a small thicket. Oweka followed them but he did not pass through the gap.

In the bush, the mother was made to kneel and the baby was put on her back. They were then bathed in the same position with very cold water mixed with herbs. The water was contained in a mortar. Each time water was splashed on the two, the baby cried and it almost stopped breathing. In Oweka's case, a lamb was put on his back and the two, man and animal, were washed. They did not dry themselves but just dressed, water still dripping from their bodies. They then hurried away to Oweka's home. Others followed them in single file. No one was to look behind, apart from one old woman who moved with ash in a calabash. She looked back at intervals, sprinkled the ash after her, slapped her private parts and raised her hands high up as though she wanted to pull the sun down. The ash would make the evil spirit blind if it wanted to follow them.

At Oweka's home, various rituals were performed. Very black soil mixed with dung was put on everyone's forehead. From then, no one was to greet anyone again. Everyone appeared serious. A big calabash of sim-sim was brought, part of it was sprinkled over the house. The rest was given to the people to chew. They chewed while abusing the mother and child. The words were so obscene that if a stranger were to appear, he would think that this was the region where wickedness originated. With them, everything was fine. An abundance of food was brought and they ate with full appetites. After that a master pot of beer was brought and people fell to drinking. This was the time when people were allowed to greet each other, to talk and smile. Old people got up and blessed the child but their blessings were restricted. They were not allowed to mention death or evil spirits, it was a sign of inviting them. One old man got up.

"I would like to thank all of you," he started, "for your presence here. It is very, very encouraging to see all of you gathered here to pray for the life of a little one. We are soon dying and we want people who can take over. The gods I know have listened to our prayer and observed our desperate actions. They will answer us in the way we need it." He sat down and everyone agreed that he had spoken sense. Another old one, a woman, got up.

"I was a very hard working, clean woman so I hope the child will follow my ways." She spat on her palms and smeared the child's feet with her saliva. Her hands were very rough and they must have scratched the child. An old man got up. He had all along been eager to talk and he shot up before the old woman had finished.

"My only prayer as an old one is that the great one may bless our labours." He turned towards the mother and child. "My grandchild, you have been born, we have prayed to the great one, you will live, the other is to wait for death..." This last sentence provoked everyone around. The old man was shouted down and forced to sit immediately. People grumbled. This was very bad from an old man like him. He very well knew the enemy and yet he smiled at it. If it was not for Oweka, the old man would have been torn into pieces, but Oweka being the host wanted less trouble.

And so, the name Adirisa was given to the girl. It was symbolic, meaning "Through the Window." She had escaped from death through the window and whether it was this act or a mere coincidence, no one knows but Adirisa Maria came to live, to become what she became.

Unfortunately for Oweka, his wife did not get pregnant again. It was as if that evil spirit said, "OK, you have managed to make that one live but you'll never get another one, not even one that will die after two days." Oweka wanted children, he never wanted only one child. What if Maria were to die, he would remain empty-handed again. Oweka was disturbed by this. More so, Maria was a girl. If she had been a boy, he would not have worried so much. Maria would get married somewhere some day. When he died, who would take up his name? His wife was even getting old and there was no hope of getting another child. His relationship with Mama Maria started dwindling, their life became complicated. He waited for another child, a boy child, but he was never fulfilled. He started finding mistakes in everything his wife did. Her

16

cooking was bad, her dress was beshaming, her walk was mad, her bedroom was stinking. Her all and her whole were not Oweka's choice. She was pain, never a wife to him anymore. He cursed why he married her.

Mama Maria became bothered and tired of Oweka's curses. It seemed Oweka took it for granted that she was deliberately refusing to produce. She considered herself completely innocent. It was not her choice, she was being driven by nature. "If it is man responsible, then let him make me have a baby," she thought and wanted to tell him this but she feared. It would be playing with fire. Oweka was always right and wise. More so, she was more or less childless, therefore she had no standing in Oweka's compound. But the more he cursed the more she felt the burning desire to tell him the reality. It was too much for her. Oweka slapped and abused her when she was not wrong, he shamed her before his and her friends. She felt lost and she thought she had a right to find a place. She approached him.

"My dear," she began with a soft tone but conveying seriousness, anger, sadness and weariness. "It is not my choice to be what I am, but if you feel it is man who is able, then I give you the duty to make all possible. For my case, I don't hold anything in my palms. I am not the controller. I am controlled though I don't know the hands controlling me..." Oweka could not believe his ears. For the first time a mere woman wanted to challenge him. He slapped her several times and started shouting.

"Woman, you are simply a woman here. This is not your home, it is mine. I am the big man here, I control everything and I am the one to talk. You have no right to speak here. If you want to speak, then go back to your brothers. There you were born but here you are just a woman, married. Are my cows questioning your father? Are they failing to multiply? My cows are producing night and day and you are here filling my latrines with faeces! You think a stupid girl is of any use to me? You are of no value here. You roam, you go back to your people. Does your father send my cows to check on me? You are very stupid and next time you answer me I am going to kill you!" he jeered.

She felt like killing him but she had no energy. She felt like dying but she didn't want to leave her daughter behind. She wanted to answer him but she would be beaten. She wanted to do very many things but she could not do anything. In her mind bitter reason was turning round and round. "In my own house I am told to shut up. I am not supposed to talk because I am a woman merely married here. Matters concerning this family don't belong to me, because I am merely married. I am always stupid and wrong because I am a woman. Because I am a woman, my ideas are useless. I am to produce and wait for death in silence because I am a woman, merely married. Where I was born I am told that I am no longer concerned with their matters, that I am married somewhere else and that is where I should go and speak. They no longer want me in their affairs. I am an intruder. Where then do I belong? " She shed tears in secret and left the house.

Oweka decided to take a second wife. He could not wait any longer. His days were ticking away and yet nothing came to please him. His aim was to lead a happy life on earth but this was impossible without children. He therefore decided to take another wife.

The woman he chose seemed to have understood Oweka's problem very well. Each year she had a swollen belly. Within eight years she already had five children, three boys and two girls. At last, Oweka was fulfilled. He could afford to speak like a full man in a drinking place. Nobody ignored him, his position became safe. At night, his home would fill with the cries of children and Oweka would feel his heart rise and fall in pride, contentment and harmony. He had got a woman, he had found her. He loved her like a jewel, like he loved himself. No one could talk against her, she was right all the time.

Maria's mother became so remote to him. He never bothered whether she lived or not. He never accounted for her in his life. But she clung to Maria as the only comfort on earth. She had tried to go back to her family but her brothers sent her back. They were always proud to be attached to a rich man like Oweka. He was their pride. Besides, if she was to rejoin her family, Oweka would demand his cows. It would mean adding another burden, Maria, to them. They already had enough children to feed, so she stayed. She had to bear all kinds of suffering. Whilst she had a child to care for, she had to remain and care for Maria. She had nowhere else to go, so she stayed against her will.

A very large gap developed between Oweka's wives. He taught the first wife to adore the second one and the second wife to despise the first one. The second wife seemed to like this so much. She had too much prejudice towards Mama Maria. On rare occasions, Oweka visited Maria's mother to beat her, and whenever Maria protested he beat her too. Oweka lived with his wives like cats and dogs.

* * *

The children grew up. It was difficult to tell which was the first and last born among the children of the second wife. Nonetheless, Oweka was very proud of them. They were sent to school, but only the three boys. Oweka refused to send his three girls to school. It was not their privilege to learn. Their work was to learn how to dig, cook and later on get married. Maria's mother, unlike the second wife, would not listen to Oweka. She wanted her daughter to go to school. She knew her position so well. Maria was her only child and if she was to lead a poor life then she had no other child to look to as a source of comfort. She was very poor but she scratched everywhere to get money to send her daughter to school. She made a contract with rich Indians in the nearby trading centre. She sold them firewood at a meagre price and had to carry firewood for six months in order to pay the school fees for one term. In a year she was able to pay for only two terms. The Indians, however, realised her good intentions so they agreed to lend her money. She had to carry firewood throughout the year. Every morning she got up, went to her garden and after digging she would come back, make breakfast, eat and carry firewood to the Indians. In the afternoons, she went to the bush to collect firewood for the next day. In the evening she would go to her garden. She always slept exhausted. Oweka did not like this at all. Maria was failing to learn the ways of the kitchen and she might in future fail to get married. He tried to stop his wife from earning money but she protested bitterly. Each night, Oweka beat her to stop her but each morning she carried firewood to the Indians. Oweka gave up.

At school, Maria did so well. She showed a very keen interest in learning and she was always among the top five. She was a very good example to other girls. She became so endeared to her teachers that they were the ones who secretly encouraged Maria's mother not to give up educating her daughter. Her half-brothers on the other hand were very poor at classwork. They never cared about school and were always late. They studied Primary One until they had almost developed beards.

Oweka got tired of paying their fees without seeing any development. When he saw that Maria was doing well, better than her brothers, he decided to take over responsibility from his wife. He started paying for Maria's school fees.

One day, his children came back from school and were very amused. Oweka was milking at the time they came back but he was near enough to hear their story.

"Mother," one of them started, "the Inspector came to our school today and he entered our classroom. He was too startled to see male teachers making noise with the young children. He went cross but was too surprised to discover that they were pupils. Mother, do you know, the Inspector thought we were teachers." Their mother laughed in merriment but Oweka, who had stopped milking and was listening attentively, felt so embarrassed. After milking, he decided to call his sons together and inform them that they were to stop school and look after the cattle.

Oweka was very skilful at making others shoulder the blame even when he was responsible in one way or another. Now he started cursing why he married the second wife. She had given birth to boys all right, but what were they if they were not intelligent? They were completely useless. Things have changed nowadays Education is the key. Without education one is useless. He became so fond of Maria all of a sudden. He loved Maria's mother again and started planning to divorce the second wife.

One day, the second wife came back from the garden very tired and dragging along like a snail. She caught Oweka's attention and he felt a bitter hatred for her.

"Why are you so dirty like a leper?" he asked.

"Can't you see that I am coming from the garden?"

"But yours is too much. Can the garden make you smell like rotting fish? How can you be dirty from hair to toe?"

"Say what you want. I no longer care."

"You should care, because, I wonder, anyway I wonder why I took you for a second wife."

She turned round and looked Oweka direct in the face. Despite the fact that Oweka wanted to humiliate her, she would never fear to defend herself, whenever she knew she was right. She was known throughout the village for having a burning tongue. Everywhere she went, she was heard complaining and quarrelling. When quarrelling with other women, she would climb high on an anthill or a tree so that everyone could hear and see her. And now tired from work and being abused instead of appreciated, she stood up to defend herself.

Oweka continued, "Anyway, you can live under my roof and continue eating my food but I think it would be better if you were barren because, sincerely, your children have made no difference to my life. They are just as stupid as you are. It would have been better if you had had one brilliant child like Maria. What do you think I am going to do with these many stupid children?"

She threw the hoe down and cleared her voice. "My friend," she started.

"How can you address me as your friend?"

"OK, I am sorry, my enemy..." Oweka shook his head and waited for her words." They are not my children alone. They are mine and yours. You have a big problem which I know. You don't want to be attached to bad things, you only want to associate yourself with good ones. The good children are yours and the bad ones are for your wives. What kind of man are you? But I don't care. Outside there, they call them your sons, Oweka's sons not mine. They say Oweka's sons are stupid, they are fools. You may deny them but the world will never stop calling them yours. You can even send them away or kill them, your fellow men will say you destroyed your sons not strangers. What kind of husband are you? Sincerely I have never seen such a confused family head. You are truly stupid. Your sons must be stupid like you. Why do you blame me alone? Why don't you teach them? I thought you lived with the boys more than I do. You say you are the master of the home, why don't you teach your children sharpness? They are your children too. You cannot say they are not yours because they are not successes. Have you heard...?"

She was talking at the top of her voice, swinging her arms high in the air. Whenever she mentioned the word 'stupid' she spat on the ground. Oweka realised she had to be stopped, otherwise she was going to create a big scene. He charged at her.

"How can a mere woman afford to answer me so? How can you abuse me in my compound? Who is the master here? Is it me? Is it you? Even my real wife cannot abuse me. Who told you to defy me?

21

You must have forgotten I am the one who married you." He hit her hard around her ears." Next time you'll learn to respect your husband."

"Amen," she replied.

Oweka was more angered. He had expected her to cry but instead got the answer "amen". He went crazy with rage and grabbed the hoe she was handling. He made to hit her with it but she was quick enough to run and Oweka made after her with the hoe poised. They raced around the compound and he was almost catching her when he heard a voice from behind him.

"Oweka, what are you doing? Don't kill that woman!" He stopped all of a sudden and turned round to find who the hell had stopped him. He was panting and his eyes had gone red. He was surprised to find that it was the priest.

"Why do you want to kill your wife?" the priest asked again.

"I don't want to kill her, sir."

"Then you wanted to beat her, I presume?"

"No I was not going to beat her."

"What where you doing then?"

"We are only playing, we were happy and felt a need to express it beyond words. Sincerely, we were playing. This hoe, I did not mean to hit her with it. It was just playing."

"That's enough my man." The priest was annoyed. It was clear to him that Oweka was lying. He turned to the woman, "Is it true, Madam?" He asked while pointing at her to make sure she understood that the question was directed at her.

She wanted to tell him the plain truth, but at the thought of Oweka's trick she smiled. "So this is how people can get out of traps?" she thought. "Yes, we were playing in the name of goodness."

Oweka sighed and he realised he had mastered her somehow. The priest relaxed. After all the victim he wanted to help was contented. He went away knowing very well that this couple was for war but they had lied to him. He knew that after his departure Oweka would not forgive his wife because she had at long last done the good job of saving his name. He would beat her all the same.

* * *

For a long time, Oweka's family continued to live under harsh treatment. His only child was Maria, the rest were the children of their mother. It was their mother who made them stupid.

"In the history of my family," Oweka would say, "we have never registered stupid men. This stupid blood must have come from the woman's home. I wish I had known they had stupid blood, I would never have taken a wife from them. If I am to marry another time, I have to learn everything about the family I am going to take a wife from. Next time, if I am not careful I might take a mad woman, ha ha ha ha!

"But after all I have one thing to please me. Maria is doing very well. Long ago, we used to underrate women but I think Maria has shattered that tradition. I know she is going to be a great woman in future, don't you think so?"

That was how Oweka wanted things. Everywhere he went, in the church, in drinking places, he wanted people to talk about Maria. Any topic other than that was foolish. Education, books was Maria and none else. If people talked about other things, he whirled round and round and brought it back to his daughter. He would then begin to praise her.

"Education has truly changed things, my people. You see children carrying books and you wish you were young. I really admire my daughter Maria. I wish I were young, I would go to school with her. She has pleased me surely. I wish God had given me two such children. I would be the most contented man on earth. But God is funny, he has given me instead very stupid boys. This woman's children really bother me. They are making very stupid failures themselves."

"Oweka, I thought you went for the second wife because you wanted children. You wanted boys and you have got them. What else is disturbing you? What has gone to your head again?" Simeon would ask.

"Yes, I know that better than you. I know I wanted sons but sons do not merely mean a being with a male's genitals. There are other factors apart from the genitals that make a man or a woman. These ones are not men in any way. They are not stern, they are not hard men in character like I used to be, they are useless. Maria, though a girl, is my true child. She has the pressing spirit, she is hard working, she is like me. Those boys, ha ha, I don't know what I will do with them."

23

"Oweka, I know you are a father, but you are just a mere child to me," Simeon would rebuke him. "It's not good to say so and so is bad and so and so is good in a family. You are creating gaps between your family members. You are breaking your family into pieces. Your sons may be stupid all right but it's bad to speak it everywhere. Your sons could even be good in some other things. I know education has taken the lead but success in education does not necessarily mean success in life. You are making your sons inferior before their friends."

"But I am speaking facts, eh? These are facts. I cannot run away from it. My sons are fools and I know this very well. Even you out there know it. I am not being biased nor segregative to my children. This is what everyone knows."

"Well, you say you know better. OK, I see. Maria, which form is she in now?"

"Oh!" Oweka's heart would leap with happiness. He wanted to spread the gospel of Maria's greatness every time, everywhere." She has gone up so rapidly that I cannot also believe it myself. She is now in Senior Five," he would say confidently but in actual fact Oweka did not know what Senior Five was. In his heart he always feared that one day someone would ask him what it was. However, he was lucky that most people in the village never wanted to show their ignorance. He would always tell them and they would nod in wonderment but in ignorance.

"That's very fine. In fact, that's too good. But then, I don't understand this. After that where will she go?"

"Oh, oh, my dear, she will be going to Makerere. After this she will automatically join Makerere."

"Which, which Makerere in particular?"

"Well, I don't know, I don't know. You see these days learned ones choose very high tastes, Makerere Oxford, or Makerere USA. She might choose to go to that one of Britain."

"What is she going to become after Makerere?"

"Maria must become a doctor. Yeah, she must become a doctor, then she'll treat all of us. That will be very great. We shall never fall sick again. Education is very good. Everyone should take his children to school, then we shall get many doctors, even presidents. Don't you see that..."

"OK, OK. I understand you now. I understand you very well now."

CHAPTER THREE

Oweka kept on changing the scheme of things in his family to the extent that Maria was made the Lord of all and others adored her. In the exam year he stopped her from doing any work, claiming she had too much to read. Whenever she tried to help her mother Oweka would quarrel almost throughout the year.

"Maria go and read," he would shout, "I have married those women to work. If they can't cook or fetch water then we can stay without food. This is not what you are supposed to do. Go and read. I want you to pass. Go, let them work." Maria would go and lock herself in the room and doze off. She would get tired of reading and feel like relaxing but Oweka always forced her against her will. All the work was, however, done by his second wife and her children. They cooked, washed, did the digging and the keeping of the cattle. Oweka was their supervisor, he told them what to do, shouted abuse at them and made them desperate.

In public places, at parties and prayers, Oweka was always seen with Maria and her mother.

* * *

It was coming to Easter time again and everybody was busy preparing for the occasion. In this village, people did not know the real meaning of Easter. They knew it as a time of prayer and eating but the reason why was faint in their minds. Such occasions were celebrated by heavy drinking and much eating. A number of families would organise themselves and entertain one another in turns. This prolonged their celebrations for almost one month from what could have been done in a day. Rich people like Oweka would entertain their friends singlehanded but the poorer ones would join hands, mostly two families together, and organise as one. The first feasts always took place in rich men's homes. Today it was Oweka's family's turn to host the guests first. Oweka was therefore seen busy organising for the day.

Maria was so excited about everything and everyone wondered why. She was not a child. At her age, and with her level of education, no one expected her to get so emotionally aroused by such occasions that were repeated annually. Her stepmother thought she was being childish because she was being loved like a baby, but her mother thought that she was excited because for the first time she was going to celebrate Easter free of books. She had just finished her Senior Six examinations and she had nothing to worry about.

The long-awaited day came at last. Oweka, Maria and her mother dressed up to kill and went for prayers. Everybody admired them in the church. His other wife and her children remained at home to do the work. They were to look after the cattle and organise a sitting place for the drinking. Oweka remarked that they were too dirty to move with him.

At the church, Oweka tried to make a big show of himself. He wanted everyone to feel his presence. During the offertory, the baskets were passed round and people gave what they could. Oweka did not offer at that moment, he waited for the priest to take the big basket then he hurried to the front and pulled a bundle of notes from the trouser pocket. The priest was not pleased with it all but he could not rebuke him. It would mean losing a very prominent giver. Oweka walked back with pride as if to say "I can do it, who else?" People looked into their neighbours' eyes. That was Show Number One.

After the priest had given thanks to God for the gifts his children had offered came the time of Petition. The priest first said a general prayer, asking God to help to bless everyone. He prayed for the pagans, that one day they would see light. He then gave the rest of the time to the floor.

Daudi, who was well known for his piety, prayed first. He thanked God for the gift of His son whom He sent on earth to save sinners. "Lord we are sinners," he prayed," but your kindness is great. You sent your holy son on earth to die for poor sinners like us. Lord that is why we commemorate this day with great dedication. For without this day, we would be dead spiritual beings. Lord receive our thanksgiving. Amen."

Another old man prayed for the day to end in peace. "I know that today people are going to involve themselves in drinking but they should not fight. We should know that Jesus while on earth did not fight. He was gentle. Let's not eat too much too. For it's being greedy and Jesus condemned greed. Lord hear my prayer. Amen."

Others prayed for the sick in spirit and body, the poor materially and spiritually, the orphans, the widows, and all kinds of suffering and sufferers to be saved by God. Oweka was the last to say his petition. He thanked God for his family and for blessing him with gifts. He was a poor alien man of his people but through His love He had made Oweka a great man. He thanked God for blessing him with a wife who had given him a daughter to cherish. God had given him Maria as his everlasting joy. God truly will never disappoint His servant as long as he raises his hands up and acknowledges His saving power. He can close the doorway and yet widens the windows. His sons were wounds of shame but Maria had saved him from the shame. He talked of his great things. Thanking God for his goats, sheep, cattle, crops and the rest. He no longer feared death because he had had enough of what he wanted. Besides, he was sure his wealth would never disintegrate. Maria was the right heir God had given him... At the beginning, he sounded as if he were praying but when he gained words, no one could deny that he was praising himself.

Unfortunately, his prayer was so long and embarrassing that some people felt like walking out. Maria sank into her seat, she felt like stopping him but she could not. When he finished only a handful of people said "Amen"; the rest sighed in relief and embarrassment. The priest immediately concluded the petition because he feared another embarrassing prayer. That was Show Number Two. Very embarrassing indeed.

Oweka, however, seemed not to have realised the effect of his prayer. He went home feeling great, fulfilled and lord of all. Immediately he arrived home, things changed for the second wife. It seemed she had not done anything right since Oweka left for prayers. He found mistakes everywhere and in everything she did. This thing is not done this way, can you bring me this, do me that, what where you all along doing, this is not done ... Whenever she appeared before him, he cursed. She did everything in silence and as he said, she seemed not to care. She was used to his way of treating her but she could not believe the way things had changed. Was it really the Oweka who danced with joy when he got her? Was this really the man who promised to love her to the end? This man is surely bad, she thought.

27

She remembered when her mother told her that if she was to become a girl again, she would never get married. Her mother used to advise her to avoid married men. They take you to become unpaid housegirls to their wives. I did not follow her advice and now I am paying. She was nothing to Oweka. He regarded her like rubbish. She and her children were his servants. "But it's not me to blame, it was my father who arranged things against my will. He told me Oweka was his friend and he knew he was capable of keeping me in good shape. He said the boy I wanted was poor and if I married him I would suffer. I tried to resist but my father swore to throw me out. I married Oweka because I feared losing my home. Things worked out in the beginning as my father said but whatever happened next, only the devil knows."

People started gathering around. They came with straws, more eager to drink than eat. Oweka ordered his wife to lay lunch. Mountains of bread and soup covered with oil was served. They fell to, eating heavily. After the lunch, a huge pot of beer was brought. They sat round it and started sucking greedily. In this village people loved local brew more than anything. A man would give his neighbour food freely but it would cost more for him to offer drink. They were the most greedy people when they were drinking and they were the most generous people when they were eating. It was better for a thief to steal a man's money but not his brew.

They sucked quietly for fear of being cheated. It was clearly seen that each one wanted to drink more than the rest. Those who came late joined without ceremony. It's said that one man was one time late for a beer party. He decided that the only way he would compensate for the loss was by sucking with all his might. He sucked until the straw burst open.

After drinking for a long time, the screws in their heads fell loose, their lips opened and let out their tongues that sawed words in the air. They talked of all kinds of things. They told stories, sang and laughed. This song makes me remember this and that. They were now talking about the past and mainly how youths were treated.

"What I hate was how they treated their daughters," one woman commented.

"How did they treat them?" a man asked.

"It was bad. It was bad. The worst thing was when a girl conceived before getting married."

"What could be done?"

"It depended upon the case. To get the boy who did it, an anthill would be dug out. When the ants were exposed the girl would be thrown into it. The ants would bite here. Some ended up dying."

"What would then be done to the responsible boy?"

"The father of the girl would go to the boy's home at dawn and plant a spear in the courtyard. It was a symbol for the boy's father that his son had caused trouble somewhere. The people of the girl would gather in the boy's home the next day to resolve the problem. If the boy accepted he was the one responsible, he would be given the girl, but if he denied, the girl's stomach would be ripped open to remove the unwanted child. She would of course end up dying. Some people preferred taking her to a cliff where she would be thrown down and there she would end."

"Did most boys refuse responsibility?"

"It depended on the boy. Some boys would never like seeing their girls killed but others never cared."

"But that was right," one man recommended. "It was a way of preventing pregnancies that are unwanted. I cannot imagine my daughter getting pregnant when she is unmarried."

"I don't also encourage pregnancies before marriage but the thing I discourage is punishing the girl alone. The stupid part of it is that parents always encouraged their boys to have premarital sex and yet they tied their girls. The boys would obviously strive hard to dig girls from their hiding holes because they can't have sex without women. It would be wise to discourage both or otherwise the boy should also be punished. Didn't he know they were not married?"

"But that is not a thing to hate. That was a way of controlling girls," one old man mentioned. "The real thing to hate was their dances."

"Yeah!" a young man echoed strongly. "My grandmother told me they would always end up fighting. Some men would even be killed."

"It's good you have never seen the fights," the old man continued, "Otherwise, you would never feel like looking back at the time. I was fifteen years old when I witnessed my first and last one. At that time, there was a very beautiful girl up in the next village. Various boys wanted her but they failed, apart from two boys who never gave up. One from this village and the other from the girl's village. These two boys hated each other because each one thought that it was the other who was leading to his failure. One day, the boy from the other village planned with his friends and beat our boy seriously. The matter therefore became an inter-village dispute. When the boys had reached the peaks of their struggle and no one seemed to be winning, a dance was advertised. We all saw a fight ahead because of this dispute and we started getting ready.

"The dances those days were great. A man had to jump up high and come down with legs almost cracking the earth. He would then attract the admiration of women. The best dressed man would tuck ostrich feathers round his plaited hair, wrap a hide around his waist, jingle bells around his ankles and the rest of the body would be covered with beads. Powerful men would carry dried meat in small bags. The bags were very dirty anyway. They would chew as they danced. Some gluttons I understand over-ate so that they would belch near their girls. The girls would scatter away from them. They would later on be beaten by their mates for bringing shame to their group. But it seems I am not going on well. I am losing the story. Where was I? Where was I? Mmm-mm.

"Yeah, the dance was just advertised and we were preparing for war. It was at such dances where villages would prove masterhood over a disputed issue. At last, the day came. My mother forced me to go. For when would I prove my manhood? she asked. I was already big, she remarked. I went. Out of pressure from my mother but not choice. I feared these dances so much. The stories I had heard about them never encouraged me at all. We reached the scene and I was even more frightened. The number of people. Oh, it was as if the whole world had gathered together. Everyone was speaking, their voices gathered together and rose up like a great storm coming. One had to shout as loud as possible near their friends' ears. At times you could not hear your own voice. It was great indeed. A whistle was blown from within and immediately the whole earth fell silent. It was as if God had arrived. They knew their discipline very well. Drums then started rolling, women ululated, everyone got to his feet and dust rose from the ground like brown smoke. It was choking. I thought I would remain watching but everything entered my heart and I found myself trying the strokes of the beat. Men started sweating and their women busied round wiping for them. The drums reached the tempo of their rhythms and the men were almost breaking their legs. The women were moving their waists to and fro, to and fro like pliant reeds in a storm. Immediately the men shot up.

They were lifted high on shoulders. I was later on told that these were the leaders of village dance groups. They were up, dancing with their heads and arms. They shook their feathered heads and the feathers exaggerated everything so that women ran mad with emotion. They shook their heads, stretched their arms as though they wanted to gather the whole people to their breasts. Then a man would hold his waist in pride, push his left hand in his dirty bag, pick the meat. The right hand would grope for a handkerchief to clean his face, push back the handkerchief and he would resume dancing while chewing. They were great men of their time.

"But the men to pity were the carriers of the dancing men. They had too much difficulty in carrying loads that swayed, loads that got excited and gave extraordinary strokes. One could clearly see the muscles of the carriers' backs stretching beyond their limits. They would stagger as if they wanted to collapse but what helped them was their pride. When a man does something out of pride, he can achieve what he would never have done if he were humble, with the same amount of energy.

"The fight followed. I was not keen enough to see what started it. It was sincerely the bitter part of the sweet everything. Clubs flew in the air and women ran behind their men to encourage them to 'show them today'.

"I was still wondering how a tongue can be so long when I saw a man attacking my father. I pictured my father dead like those unlucky men and I made to help him kill the enemy. Before I could do anything, the man lifted a thick club and was about to hit me. My father ran to my rescue but I was already finished. My people, I felt weak and my knees started yielding. I realised however, that if I delayed, disaster was moving faster. My father would have to defend both me and himself and in the process one of us or both of us would perish. I gathered the little energy that enabled me to jog out of the scene, but I was pissing after every one hundred metres." This amused the people and they laughed for some time before the old man could resume.

"No, I would never go back there again, I swore. I ran home and failed to witness it to the end. However, we were beaten."

"So some people died?" a woman asked.

"Yes."

"I would never have gone to such things," a young man said.

"Oh, my son, when these men came back from their dances, they would be very aggressive and the village cowards would suffer, they would be beaten terribly. You would suffer worse than if you went. It was real bad to be a coward."

"Then I am blessed not to have existed at that time."

"Yes, Yes." Everyone agreed with the young man.

"It's good education has come and has altered things," Oweka contributed.

"Oh Oh Oh, Oweka," Simeon started, "Education is good nowadays but during the time it had just started it was simply fun. I was a boy then."

"Tell us, Simeon, is it true even grey-haired old people were forced to go to school?"

"Yes, you see, when the white man came, he introduced very many of his ways and forced us to abandon our ways. He introduced second names, western names, given by performing a ceremony of sprinkling water on heads. He was the one who united woman and man together in his church and proclaimed that man and woman were equal. That his God regards both sexes as the same. Somehow, I did not like it and I did not agree with it. How can that be? We are always men and women remain women. There is no sameness. Well, let it be. That was him and this is me. I talked of baptism, I remember. Before that water was sprinkled on your head, you had to undergo an education. We never liked it but somehow we were pushed and pulled to it. We studied with our grandparents. It was unfortunate that their heads were too dull to retain even simple things and yet it was said that one would get baptism only if one crammed what was taught. Some of the old people died before knowing anything and they would be baptised when dead. We had our lessons in the church and they ran until mid-day. We used to carry roasted cassava for our lunch. The white man provided drinking water.

"One morning, the priest introduced another topic. It was about sacraments. Whatever they are. He made us repeat the word 'sacraments' several times. At first our tongues would tie and the word never came but after constant repeating we managed. Then he proceeded to tell us that there were seven sacraments. We had to count up to seven then were left to relax. Then the priest came back to try and see whether it had stuck to our minds that there were seven sacraments. He asked us the same question: How many sacraments are there? He first questioned the old ones. It was an old man first.

'Tell me pa, he approached with gentility and exaggerated piety, How many sacraments are there?'

'Oo Oh,' he started with the voice of someone who is ever patient, 'We were only two boys and the only children of our parents. Now that the younger boy has died I am the only one who has remained.' He was touching his fingers to make sure he solved the arithmetic without error. 'Now that I have remained alone, I am suffering a lot, I have no blanket, I sleep near the fire, but I understand the kingdom you are going to take us to is for the poor and there we shall be kings. Oh what a number of kings there will...'

"OK, OK," the priest stopped him. He had already lost his temper but because he had always stressed the need for patience and love, he had to endure for the sake of setting a good example. For us, we were amused but we feared the priest. We kept the laughter to ourselves for after lessons. The priest moved to the next learner. This was an old woman.

"'Mom, how many sacraments are there?'

'Hii Hii my son,' she started, smiling, confident and as if mocking the priest for asking such a simple question. We saw in the eyes of the priest happiness and joy. At least he had got one among the old flock. She continued, 'My son, they are under my cassava garden.' Everyone in the classroom laughed and the priest was so disappointed. He could not control himself any more so he decided to warm the brains of the old ones by making them run around the churchyard. They got up, stretched themselves and started all at once to hurry. It was not running, it was hurrying around the church. Their walking sticks led the way and their legs followed. Some of them fell flat on the ground, scraping the ground with their teeth and rising with mouthfuls of grass..."

Everyone who was drinking laughed. Their tongues loosened and all of them started talking without anyone listening. Simeon had no space to talk any more. They started forming groups and each group discussed various aspects of their knowledge. Maria, who had all along sat quietly near her mother and listened to the stories with keen interest, felt bored. It was now noise reigning and it irked her. Then she remembered she had something to fulfil and she might be late. She excused herself and went to her room.

In her room, tension seized her. She was not going to sleep. She looked at her watch and it was ten o'clock. The night was in full control of the world. If she delayed, she might be too late. She had wanted to leave at the end of the party but this seemed impossible because the beer promised to take them up to morning. She was going to take the risk. She had a burning desire that would not allow her to wait. She must fulfil her mission, her appointment. But how was she going to do it? She lay down but her mind was wandering in the wilderness. She got up and tried to sit but her legs itched. She moved from one corner to another, touching this and that, hating the party outside and praying that some miracle would happen and send them away.

She turned to the window, opened it carefully, making sure it did not make any noise. She started outside. The clouds had cleared from the face of the moon and everything looked bright and beautiful, the shadows from the trees decorated the world and it was as if something greater was soon to come. Her heart lifted and she felt a string being tied round her heart and pulling her outside. No she was not going to wait. "Let come what may," she said aloud and turned immediately to dress. The window was still open, the moonlight provided enough light and she needed no candle. She changed hurriedly, got her handbag and turned to the window. Then she realised she was wearing high-heeled shoes. People would hear her. She turned back and changed to simple shoes. Again she remembered she had not fastened the door, she headed for it and made sure it was fully locked. She looked round the room to make sure everything was as ordinary as ever. When she was satisfied she turned to the window again.

She stood there for some time. Now that she had chosen to go, the conflict in her heightened. She knew she could not convince herself to remain yet she feared something wrong might happen if she went. The noise of the party was increasing every moment. She decided that she would go. The noise and the night would swallow her up and no one would discover anything. After all, they would be very busy drinking and would not miss her. Her parents would think that she was reading. "Let me go!" she said aloud. After making sure no one was watching, she opened the window wide and slipped out. She closed it after her and hurried out of the compound, making sure she was not seen. She entered the bushes and fear vanished. She felt confident, safe and sure. She gathered herself and hurried away to catch up with time. Behind her, she could still hear those men at home shouting, calling each other names and abusing their friends in obscenity. Let them have their fill, I will have mine too, she thought.

It was not a long walk before she reached the spot where he was waiting. He was standing under a tree, a shadow, partly visible. At first Maria was frightened and she was about to run, but he whispered her name and she approached him. He was a big man, almost the age of Oweka.

The moon shone on his bald head. It was the bald head that restricted his movements at night. Whether it was true or false, most people told him that witchdoctors killed his type because they used the bald heads for magic. He was much taller than Maria and he needed to bend his neck to look at her when she was close. Now, she stood near him and he bent and looked at her, like a headmaster and a pupil. In his presence, Maria felt very small. She was the first to speak.

"Jimmy, are you tired?" Her question left him without direction.

"Tired of what?"

"Tired of waiting, waiting for me?"

He didn't answer. In the first instance, she had offended him by calling him Jimmy and now she asked many questions. On second thoughts he talked.

"I was almost giving up, yes, but a man who wants never gives up. I don't mind waiting for ages here, Maria. What I care about is seeing you. The problem is not how long I wait, the thing is what I get in the end. Now that you are here everything is all right and fulfilled."

"Thank you."

"Good manners! But what made you come at this hour? You made me almost freeze here."

"I am very sorry, Jimmy, but you know I have to take care because if we are discovered we might suffer the worst."

"Don't mind that, you are in safe hands. We shall go now. We are going to walk, you know?"

"Take it easy."

"You don't mind?"

"No,"

"Good! I feared to drive in the night, besides this road is not for cars. Perhaps I can carry your bag for you."

"If you won't get embarrassed carrying a woman's bag. But after all, it's night, no one will see you and even if they see you, none can cane you for it," she said handing over the bag to him at the same time.

"Then I won't help you," he said proudly and refused the bag. She hung the bag back on her shoulder and led the way. After a short walk, she stopped all of a sudden.

"What is wrong?" he asked.

"You lead the way. I don't like it, I fear it."

He accepted at once, without hesitation. However, silently he was wondering whether girls were all that cowardly or they merely pretended in order to achieve a certain objective. Perhaps they wanted men to feel great. To feel that women depended on them for protection. Maybe they wanted to generate more love from the men. Perhaps by doing that they would feel more beautiful and tender.

Jimmy stopped all of a sudden and held Maria by the hand, pulling her to his side. Together, they walked close to each other, silently, each one having different thoughts. Maria was thinking about her parents. Her stepmother was now very busy boiling water for those drinking. Her real mother was seated quietly near her father, sucking beer and in her mind, she believed Maria was reading because that was what she told her when she begged to leave. Her father could be talking at the top of his voice, maybe praising Maria. "They don't know," she said aloud, but Jimmy was deep in thought and he didn't hear her. He was too eager to reach home. He was wondering what had happened to the distance. It seemed it had lengthened and he started longing for wings; he wished he had risked driving. His mind was very far away and he did not realise he was taking Maria at a breathless speed.

They entered the little trading centre, two lovers, yearning to hold each other more than they were now doing. Jimmy's heart lurched and he felt his knees trembling. He knew he had to hurry otherwise he would create a scene. He doubled the already fast speed. Maria pulled herself free. He stopped. "What's wrong?" he asked.

Maria replied, panting, "I am tired, I am breathless."

"You are very lazy Maria. This has been a very short walk and you

36

already complain of fatigue."

"It's not the distance, it's the speed."

"You mean I have been too fast?"

"Didn't you realise it?"

"No! I am sorry then ,but it would have been better if you pressed on and you would get rest in my house rather than here in the bush."

"No let it be here." She bent and held her knees with both hands, the handbag dangling from her shoulders. She remained in this position for about two minutes and then offered to go. She walked for a few metres and then stopped.

"What is wrong again?" Jimmy asked angrily and impatiently.

"Don't you think people will recognise me here and then my father will know everything by tomorrow?"

"You can have my coat then. It will disguise you and they will not know who you are and I will not tell them if they ask, but remember you should not talk. It's also easy to place one by one's voice." He said this while removing his coat and handing it over to Maria. She put on the coat and felt confident. They passed by the one street of the trading centre almost in stealth. The houses here were iron-roofed but with very old iron sheets that had acquired brown as their own colour. The whole centre was punctuated by music here and there. Everyone was celebrating the miracle of the dead rising. In open places, people were seen dancing and in dark corners they were seen in twos. Jimmy and Maria moved past them and deliberately did not look at them.

There was no difference between the way of life of the people in this trading centre and that of the villages around it. The only slight difference could be that there were more houses here and they were closer together. Also this was the place where things were sold and bought. Otherwise, the rest of the things were more or less the same. Nonetheless, people here boasted that they were "city guys and chicks." They despised those in the village and often did not want to associate with them. This was where Jimmy lived. His house was at the extreme end.

It was a small house, more or less a hut. He only rented the house for a stopping point between his business trips. Otherwise he resided far away. Sometime back, he was seen in the house once in a blue moon despite the fact that he paid full monthly rent and promptly too. However, since he got Maria, he visited the house frequently, he even furnished it and made it habitable and admirable.

The two reached the home, Jimmy's home. The atmosphere here was calm. There was no music to disturb them. The only whisper came from the trees being disturbed by the wind. The moon was now holding the world in its brightness and from the tree next to the house an owl was hooting. It was if it regarded the two figures with suspicion and was telling the rest of the owls to be alert. Jimmy pushed his hand in his pocket and brought out a key. He pushed it into the keyhole and turned it; it made only a slight noise but it was enough to frighten the owl. It flew just some few metres above the roof and landed on a tree not very far from the one it had left. If it was running away from danger, then it had made a meaningless progress. The two however took little notice. They were absorbed in themselves.

Jimmy pushed the door and it gave way readily. He stepped in first and murmured, "Come in. You are welcome to my dusty bachelor's house, Maria."

"Thank you. I thought I told you I too like dusty rooms," she replied while following him. She found it dark inside and she halted all of a sudden.

"Please come in. Come, come," Jimmy wooed her. He took her hands and led her straight to his room. "You can sit on the bed. There are no chairs here you know." She sat as she was told. He then gazed lighting the lamp. After he had finished, he sat on a very low stool so that he was directly under Maria's nose. He raised his head and started at her with half-closed eyes, as if trying to find a solution to a puzzle, as though he had not placed her, as though there was something about her he had not discovered. Maria turned her eyes away. From the corner of her eye she could see that he was still gazing. Jimmy knew this. He knew that Maria was observing him from the corner of her eye and he continued staring.

He had very big features. A big nose, swollen eyes, drooping lips .... He had been modelled with too much material. The maker must have been an extravagant one. But now that a combination of big sub-features were combined to make one huge feature, he did not look unfair. In fact, in Maria's school he would have been described as a 'there, there' man. He was not handsome, not ugly, but he was just 'there, there'. He was the type you would never fear to introduce to a friend nor would you feel proud and confident taking him to a beauty contest. Indeed he was a 'there, there' fellow. Even in the lamplight, one could see that his shoes were having trouble containing his feet. They were swollen with content and rested solid on the ground.

Now Maria was feeling uneasy and she prayed that he would turn his eyes away from her. He didn't. She felt shy and started playing with her fingers, she found no strength in playing with her fingers, she buried her chin in her palms and stared at the wall. Her legs started shivering. Jimmy stared even harder. She could not hold it any longer, tears approached. Jimmy smiled as he got up, Maria sighed faintly. He set a bottle of beer before her.

"Please drink for your health and mine."

"Thank you," Maria said and lowered her head. He lit a cigarette and started smoking. They did not talk and the atmosphere was tense for Maria. Jimmy finished his first cigarette, opened the window and threw the butt outside.

"That's how people cause fire accidents," Maria commented.

"Mine will not." He took another cigarette. When he was lighting it he realised Maria had finished her drink. He picked up the empty bottle and got a full one and resumed his smoking. Maria drank as though it was water. Within no time she had done away with the second bottle. Jimmy gave her a third one but she did not touch it. She was already dizzy, a sip would have made her dead drunk. Jimmy finished his second cigarette and this time threw the butt down and stepped on it. He turned on the music. Then he moved close to Maria and held her in his arms. Whatever that musician was thinking when he composed that song no one knows. The music was low and the man singing had a sleepy voice, his words reached the heart like rain from heaven after a great period of drought. It seemed he had been dozing when he played the song. Jimmy laid Maria's head on his lap, he lowered his head as if to kiss her but only put his lips on hers and remained in that position for a while. He laid her tenderly on the bed and his lips followed hers. He kissed her. He caressed her and she felt hot, she felt cold, she did not know exactly what she felt. He started fumbling with her skirt. She held her skirt tight and made to protest.

"No-oo-oo, " Maria whispered.

"You are my love. Why do that? Why do it to me? I love you. It's only love, I mean no harm. Feel free, trust me. I only love you. Let me have time, Maria?" She could not resist any more. Whenever she was with him, she lacked the courage and the strength to resist. "Maria, I love you. Why can't you trust me?"

"How much do you want me to trust you Jimmy?"

"Maria!" She did not respond to him by words but just moved close to him." Why do you like calling me Jimmy?'

"It's your name I thought."

"It's my name all right, but it does not please the ears and heart when you mouth it. Maria, say Daddy, say 'I trust you Daddy', not Jimmy."

"I trust you Jimmy."

"Maria say 'I do Daddy'. She giggled and kept quiet. "Maria," Jimmy said seriously, "Say 'I do Daddy'. She still kept quiet. He pinched her hard and she almost shouted at the top of her voice, "I do Daddy!"

"Maria, why do you need to be pushed into doing everything? For just a mere word, Daddy, you have to be pinched." Maria kept quiet, Jimmy held her close. "Maria, I love you. Don't get annoyed with me, don't cry, it was mere play. I love you. Do you love me too? Say it, come on, Maria."

"I do love you Daddy." Her voice was trembling. He kissed her, his heart was thundering. He kissed her hard and caressed her hot. He kissed her again and again. She felt weak all over, her head was thick and she could not think any more. The only words that she could understand were "I love you, I need you." He kissed her. He lay her flat on her back and eased off her panties. The last words she heard from him were "Show me then, show me that you love me." He found his way and they were soon gone to faraway lands, to where only the two of them knew...

They were now sleeping. Maria was sound asleep and completely relaxed. She looked very innocent in her sleep. Jimmy was dreaming. He was walking home from a neighbour's. In reality, the distance was only a stone's throw away but today, he was walking and walking but he was not getting there. He could see the roof of their kitchen yet he could not reach it even after a two-hour walk. He was tired and he gave up. He sat down to rest, then he discovered he had arrived. But it was not home again. He was on a lake shore. What had brought him here? The shore was lonely and the sun had just set. Beasts could be heard roaring from behind. Fear overcame him, he tried to run but his legs were paralysed. He looked back and found a small bird looking at him. It was small, lonely and cold. He admired it and wanted to get it, he didn't care about the beasts any more. He stretched out his hand but he could not reach it. He stretched again, this time more than the first time, but it was in vain. OK, I am going to try for the last time, he told himself. He then stretched so hard, beyond his limits, but caught it by the tail. Carefully he brought it closer, fearing that the feathers would come out and leave the bird free. He was so pleased with his efforts. He had got something to love in a place where fright was the only friend. He turned round trying to find an escape route with his new love, but instead discovered that the sun was rising, not setting.

Fear had left him, he looked at the bird, it was not a bird, it was Maria. She was in his arms, staring at him, expecting something from him. She looked completely innocent. She was smiling. He became so excited and wanted to take Maria home with him. He held her tight and started hurrying... But his home was again at the opposite shore. He did not remember crossing the lake, but how did he reach here? He realised he had fallen in shit. No one was nearby to help. There was no boat on the shore he would have crossed with Maria. He was puzzled. Then in frustration, he approached the shore, Maria in his arms. What he saw embarrassed him. It was not a lake, it was merely a stream that would take two strides to cross. It was very shallow, as shallow as a plate. No fishes lived in the water, he only saw toads swimming at the bottom of the water. He stepped in the water with one foot and found that he could cross easily. He lifted Maria on his shoulders and started off.

In his mind, he was wondering why he was looking for a boat where boats were not needed. Then all of a sudden, the stream became so deep and it became so wide, the water was rising every minute and it reached his neck. How foolish he was to try to cross a lake on foot! He tried to go back but he could not trace his way. Besides, they were now in the centre, the distance behind them and before them was the same. There was no point in walking back. The lake was too quiet and too dark. No one was fishing. The only noise came from hissing animals that sent a chill to his heart. He tried to cling to the weeds in the lake but they were too frail. Then he saw some people on the shore. They looked very small and he could not tell what they were doing. He summoned them.

They saw him but did not bother and continued doing their work. It seemed they could not understand him. He decided to cry for help. They heard but simply ignored him. They were bad men. He had to find a solution. He had to save himself and Maria. But how would he do it? Then he started swimming, groping for his way with Maria on his shoulders. Again a big storm case from nowhere and he could not swim anymore. Maria became so heavy that he could not breathe. What was he going to do? Both of them could not die. At least one should die and the other should survive. He decided to drop Maria. He saw her going deep under the water. She did not cry, she did not tell him anything, not goodbye, not even a desperate plea for help, but in her eyes he read all these and even more beyond. In her eyes, he saw her blaming him, blaming him for carrying her from the shore only to drop her in the middle of the lake. He had betrayed her. He saw hatred in her eyes but he could not tell how much she cursed him. He saw all the ill feelings one can have for an enemy. But it was done. Let it be. He swam and almost reached the shore when he woke up. He was breathless and completely frightened. He tried to get up. Someone was shaking him.

"Who are you? Who is here?"

"Daddy, what's wrong?" Oh, it was Maria. So she had not sunk after all, it was only a dream. He sighed in relief.

"What is wrong?" Maria asked again.

"Nothing very wrong. I have only been dreaming."

"What was the dream?"

"It was not so great a dream but at least it was about you."

"What about it?"

"Nothing great I say, I dreamt that I love you," he lied. "I wanted a better dream."

"What can be better than that?"

"Your living by my side forever! Don't you think so, Maria?"

"I can't tell exactly. That's your best. Mine could be different."

"Which one is yours then?"

"To be loved sincerely."

"Maria, up to now you still don't believe that I love you?"

"You may love me but not sincerely."

"Why?"

"I know I am not alone, you could be having another woman somewhere."

"Maria, when will you learn to trust me?"

"I just don't need to learn it. It's your job to convince me. You are blindfolding me but I know I am not alone. You know that too. Jimmy, instead of lying why don't you leave me alone if you can't love me alone?"

"Maria, you are a very complicated woman. Is that why you woke me up? Did you wake me up to quarrel with me?"

"No, I want to go back home."

"Not now. I can't escort you now, it is still too early."

"I want to go!" She was rude and she was trembling.

"Maria, it's very hard to leave you. It's very hard to say bye to you. You know I love you so, please take it from one; you are alone. I love no other girl and I have no wife despite my age. I thought I explained to you why I am single. You are alone. If at all I had a wife, I don't think I could spend this day here with you and leave my wife and children. Maria, I have spent great days with you. If I had had a wife it would not have been possible. Please have trust and believe me." Maria kept quiet. He touched her naked body, it was warm and welcoming. He kissed her and she responded. She did not resist. It was sweet being with her, she was heaven. Oh Maria... She moaned faintly...

"Jimmy, let me go now."

"I will let you go. Are you longing for home so much?"

"I have a feeling I should go."

"Get up and dress than." She got up immediately. Jimmy remained lying on the bed, he was feeling lazy. He knew outside was cold yet Maria wanted to drag him to it. He closed his eyes and wished Maria was back at his side. Maria finished dressing and she took her handbag and turned to Jimmy.

"Get up and let's be going." He instead turned round and pulled the blanket over his head. Maria pulled the blanket off and threw it on the floor. "Jimmy get up or I go alone." He got up slowly, dressed as if he had thorns in his clothes. He sat back on the bed, yawned and pulled Maria close to him. "Maria, let's live together like this forever, don't go."

"Jimmy, let me go. Remember we are not legally recognised. Daddy, please let me go." He got up at once, took the bag from Maria and led the way. Maria followed hurriedly. He opened the door and they stepped out. The moon was sinking and they had to hurry. They followed the path they used for coming and soon left the trading centre behind them.

* * *

Immediately Maria had left the drinking place, Oweka and Simeon picked up an argument. They had started simply by describing the marvels of creation. The high mountains, the great lakes, all that water, oh it was indeed great. Then Oweka without much thought told Simeon that what puzzled him was that the earth was round and it rotated. Simeon asked him to explain but Oweka could not. Obviously Simeon rejected the theory.

"Oweka, how can you tell me that the earth is round? I have walked miles and miles and I have never found any slope like that of a ball. I am old in this world, you are only a child of yesterday. I know more than you do."

"Simeon, you are older, but I am wiser." They disagreed on the point but they had no reasons to support their sides. They simply kept on saying, "I know better," until they could say it no more. Oweka had learnt that the earth was round from Maria. He very much wanted to win the argument and he realised that the only way was to get Maria to explain. He would even feel proud. He had seen Maria leaving but he hadn't seen her come back. He rushed to the house and headed for Maria's room. He knocked on the door, called Maria but he received no response. The room looked dark. Oweka pressed his ear against the door but he could not hear any noise. He banged the door and called out louder. He was so drunk that he couldn't think. He leaned heavily against the door and tried to get his brain to work. He decided to try the window. He tried the first window, but he received no response.

He fell into a state of panic. Something had happened to his daughter. Maybe Maria had committed suicide? Maybe some malicious hands had done away with his daughter. So everyone here was against his daughter. So these men had been eating his food and drinking his beer yet in their hearts they had planned malice. "They are joking, they will see, they will know that I am Oweka. I will teach them."

He moved to the next window, just above Maria's bed and hit it. It gave way. "These people have kidnapped my daughter," he said aloud. His head cleared and his brain worked at full speed now. He climbed through the window into the room. He started groping for anything that could provide light. He found a box of matches on the table, struck one.

44

Maria was missing! He got another match and struck it, a candle was nearby and he lit it. He stood for some time, planning what to do. He decided to survey the room. He started with the door. It was locked and the key was in its hole. He went back to the centre of the room, the candle in his hand, and tried sort out what was wrong. He could not come to a satisfactory conclusion. He went back to survey the whole room. Nothing was missing. The dress she had been wearing was hanging just above he bed, even the shoes were thrown apart, the sandals had been carefully placed under her bed, the nightdress was on her bed. Everything was in order. He started asking himself: "Do the kidnappers have time to change a dress for her?" With the candle in one hand, he climbed back through the same window. The wind was threatening to put out the candle so he curved his hand and used it as a shield against the wind. He bent low and started surveying the sand. Below the window there were fresh marks of Maria's shoes. They followed one direction, away from the compound but they did not come back. Besides hers there were no others. "There is something fishy," he concluded while nodding his head in agreement with his inner self. He climbed back into the room, the candle went out and he let it fall from his hand. He opened the door and went to the drinking group.

"Where is Maria's mother?" he asked without ceremony.

"She has gone to sleep," someone replied. He went back to the house immediately. He found Maria's mother in bed and he forced her up.

"Where is Maria?"

"Where is she?"

"Don't be a fool! I need an answer, I am not telling you to repeat after me."

"I don't understand you well."

"My question is, where is Maria?"

"She went to sleep."

"No! She is not sleeping. I am just from her room and she is missing."

"Then I can't tell."

"You know. You were the last person she spoke to. She must have told you where she was going."

"She told me she was going to sleep and that's what I have all along been knowing. If she is missing, I have no idea."

"If she's gone to one son of a bitch, I will see then."

45

"Stop making silly conclusions. Maria may be somewhere else. How can you come to such a conclusion so soon?"

"Woman, you can't say I am silly! Eeeh? You were with your daughter and you must have planned this together."

"I am not saying you are silly, I am only cautioning you for being rushy. You might later on regret your action."

"I don't care about that. Say what you want, I only want to know where you daughter is." His wife kept quiet. Oweka felt bitter. It seemed to him she was fooling him. "Can't you tell me where your daughter is?"

"Oweka, I told you I don't know."

He slapped her so hard. She was taken unawares, she screamed like a piglet, running round the room and knocking things down. Those who were drinking fell into panic. They wanted to know what was wrong. Their legs were however working independently from their brains and therefore they could not reach the scene. They just kept on milling around within, falling down and breaking the chairs and tubes. Simeon, who had talked a lot throughout, was not drunk and he was able to reach the scene first. He found Oweka strangling his wife.

"Hey! Oweka, you are going to kill her!" he shouted while pulling Oweka off his wife. "What is wrong?"

Oweka was panting hard. He glared at his wife like a greedy dog. "She ... she ... she is stupid, very stupid indeed. She is rubbish." He stopped short.

"Why is all this?" Simeon asked.

"Instead of telling me the truth, she is fooling me."

"What truth?'

"Her daughter is missing and she knows where she is but she can't tell me."

"Is it true you know where Maria is?"

"Simeon, sincerely, I don't know where she is. Oweka is only mistreating me because I am Maria's mother and because ..."

"Keep quiet!" Oweka cut her short. "I saw you planning from the drinking place and you thought I was not seeing. You are a bitch. You and your daughter."

"Oh, Oweka, that's too much." Simeon exclaimed. "Your wife may be innocent. Why can't you agree with her? Where do you think Maria is gone?"

"She is with a son of a bitch and her mother knows. I know what women are but they will know me..." Oweka was shouting at the top of his voice. A few other men had managed to compromise their legs with their brains and were now standing around the scene, their eyes wide open and round like balls. They stared at the same place without understanding anything. Their heads seemed too heavy for their necks, their heads weighed down their necks. Their lips parted and saliva slobbered like babies'.

Simeon remained quiet for some time before he resumed talking. "Oweka, this is what you should do: leave your wife alone. This is not the right time to settle such a problem. Be patient and wait for tomorrow..."

"Yes, yes, yes." Those who were standing agreed in chorus. Then one man who was standing there craned his neck and talked. He was very drunk. "It's now beer acting, it's not Oweka, let him be patient. We shall be able to help him tomorrow."

Oweka felt demeaned. "How can he tell me they will help me solve my domestic problems as if I am not a man in my home? I will show them I am very contented without them." He lifted the chair and shouted. "Everybody get out of here before I hit your arses, you are smilers with daggers. You aided Maria. She is with one of your sons, sons of your wives, your wives who are bitches! Why does she do that when you are here? Why didn't she make it any other day but today? I say go away, I don't want to see you here. You drink my beer and urinate all over my compound yet your hearts plan to cut my throat. Go! Go away all of you. This is my home and no one can claim to be above me. How can you say you are going to help me as if I am not a man? Go!"

Simeon was the first to leave. Some other men also followed him quietly and left for their homes. The rest refused to go. They went and resumed drinking happily as though nothing had happened. They were determined to drink until morning.

Oweka came out and saw them. "What about the rest of you? Do you have ears?" Oweka asked, but they continued drinking, pretending they had not heard anything. This added to Oweka's anger. He ran towards them, picked up a chair and hit the pot hard. It broke, exploding like a bomb. Everyone took to his heels at once, running in all directions. Nobody staggered. In fact, they were almost flying. Oweka jeered after them and went back into his house.

He was like a lion among other little animals. From his room, he started shouting at Mama Maria. "I will never want this nonsense of passing children through the window. You can now see how Maria still wants to do it at this age. But today, either through the window or door, you and your daughter will leave my home. You taught her to jump over windows like a monkey. You must be thinking that I am a fool but today you'll know the truth. I know from inside you, you are calling me a fool, that's why I am talking and you are just quiet. The minute is coming and you will know me better." He got up and went to his sons who were sound asleep. He woke them up.

"Come," he whispered, "I want you to help me do something, come and be quick." The boys who were still sleepy dressed hurriedly and followed their father obediently. They entered Maria's room. There he explained to them what was wrong and started instructing them on what to do. "Let's close the window and wait in here. She will come and we shall get her red-handed. No one can play tricks on me." He locked the window and started pacing round the room, then all of a sudden he stopped, he pushed his hand in his pocket, then he stared down for a little while. He changed his mind, "No, let everyone find a safe corner to hide. Hide anywhere where she cannot see you." He unlatched the window but left it closed. "This is better, she will enter thinking she is safe and we shall get her." He turned round and found a corner to hide. He stood straight and remained quiet.

They waited for five hours and it seemed ages. Oweka was feeling embarrassed. I am a fool, he thought. My daughter could be dead somewhere and I am here fussing around. He was sober now and he cursed why he had behaved rashly. My daughter is dead! He moved towards the window and was about to lock it when he heard something like a whisper. He retreated, taking care he did not make any noise. This was enough to put his sons on the alert.

Maria and Jimmy were moving together, hand-in-hand and almost tiptoeing. When they approached the window, they disengaged their hands and Maria stood in the front. She started opening the window, slowly, but with great care so that it made no noise. She spent more than two minutes doing it and Jimmy though patient was feeling nervous. He kept on glancing right, left and behind. When at last she finished, he lifted her up and she jumped in easily. She turned to face him and they kissed each other heatedly.

"Stay nice, Maria my doll," Jimmy whispered.

"Jimmy don't go. It's too nice to be with you, why don't you begin another night now?"

"How I wish I could." He kissed her again. His heart lifted and he held her neck tight as though he was going to drag her out. Something was encouraging him to follow her into the room. It was becoming so hard to leave. He felt as though he was about to part with his heart. He made as if to climb but hesitated again. 'No', his inner self told him. "Goodbye for now, my little Maria." But she kept quiet so he remained still. "Please Maria, accept this goodbye."

"Jimmy, but it's the hardest thing to do now. I cannot leave you. It's hard to say bye."

"No, we shall soon be together again. We shall soon be living together. Only stay well, be good and take care till we meet again." She buried her face in her hands and amidst tears whispered, "Goodbye."

Jimmy pulled her hands from her face and kissed them. "Goodbye, see you again." He turned and left.

Maria cried from behind him, aloud, "When shall I see you again?" He did not stop to answer, she remained standing by the window. She saw him retreat and soon he was covered by the bushes. She closed the window with care and turned towards her bed. She was about to reach it when all of a sudden, the room lit. She collapsed on the bed and covered her face. "Jesus save me," she cried. She used to hear about ghosts but she had never encountered one. She started praying with all her strength. Then Oweka's voice came from behind her. The moment she heard it she understood what her fate was.

"Yes, you have been playing the game and you thought you'd get away with it." He looked at Maria with eyes that seemed to penetrate her dress, "Where have you been you bitch?" Maria started trembling. He approached her, "Where have you been, bitch?" Maria kept quiet. "Don't you have ears?"

"Have pity on me Daddy, forgive me."

"I am not asking for any pleas. Can I know where you have been?" Still Maria kept quiet. "Have you forgotten where you have been? Or are your lips sealed?" She still didn't talk. "Okay, I will teach you how to talk." He picked a belt from the table. Instantly Maria knew what was going to follow. She raised her hand in protection while begging for mercy at the same time. He slashed her with the belt, cutting deep into the flesh of her arm. She screamed high. Her mother came running while holding her breasts and half crying. She found the door to Maria's room locked and she fell to banging it with the hope of breaking it. This made Oweka almost mad with temper. He started beating Maria and kicking her like a ball. The boys fell on him and held him tight. He tried all possible ways to free himself from their grip. He kicked in the air like a horse at its last moments but the more he fought, the more they tightened their grip on him. After realising that he could not win, he cooled down.

"Okay, you sons of a bitch, let me alone. I don't want anything less or more. Maria should leave my home!"

"Daddy where are you going to send me? Where will I go? What will I do? Please forgive me. No, I am not going anywhere. You can kill me here!" The noise at the doorway was doubling every minute. Oweka could not tolerate it any more. Maria was making unnecessary pleas, his wife was almost breaking the door and his sons still held him tight.

"Please let me get out of here," he begged his sons. "I might do something unworthy." They made sure he was calm before they let him loose. He opened the door and slapped his wife with all his might. It's difficult to tell how much pain she felt because she reacted as though nothing had happened to her. She rushed in, fell on her daughter and started crying.

"Oh Maria, what happened? Why did you do that? Why did you do it? Why? Why? Why?"

"You fools," Oweka shouted, "do you get what I mean? Maria should leave my home right now. You have chosen the ways of a bitch, go forth and practise it wherever you can, I don't entertain harlots in my house. Go and practise it somewhere else. Do you understand me? I say pack your things and go!"

Maria remained seated. How could she go? Where would she go? To Jimmy? As who? His wife? "No, I am going to die here." She felt a hatred for Jimmy. He was her hell. If not that, he made her hell. She wanted to beg for pardon but she could not. Oweka had made up his mind. He shouted at the top of his voice and her mother was wailing. She did not know what exactly to do. Oweka was threatening to come back and beat her. Then all of a sudden an idea flashed in her mind: it was as if something was advising her, could be her guardian angel. "Why, why continue to live where you are not wanted? Your father will never pardon you. Don't waste time pleading. It's like ploughing a rock. Oweka does not want you any more and there is no other choice. Though you have begun to hate Jimmy, he is the only one who can open his door for you. Your father is serious in his resolution. Turn to Jimmy as your last resort, for now, he has not sent you out of his home. If he rejects you ,you'll find what to do. Whatever problem on earth, there is always an end to it. It may end bringing joy, pain or even death but at least it's an end." She made up her mind. "I will go to Jimmy, there is no other way, I will go to him, I will go, I will!" But she did not get up to go.

Her mother was crying and advising her not to go. She begged Maria on her knees. "Please my daughter don't go, where will you go? Let him kill you, I will die with you. Oh my God! Why did I suffer under Oweka. My only child! I built to lose." She looked directly into Maria's eyes, her eyes bearing sadness, and her heart broke the deeper.

Then another voice came in. "How would you go and leave your mother? How would she live without you? Stay and comfort your mother. Why do you want to leave your mother in the hands of death? Somehow you have gone wrong. Accept your mistake and stay. You will suffer for what you did. No one else did it. Plead, Maria. Plead that your father may change his mind. Don't leave your mother!"

Maria became confused. What could she do exactly? Was she to run away from her father? Was she going to stay with her mother? She started crying and begging for pardon amidst tears. Oweka rushed in and started hurling Maria's things through the window. Everyone in the room was surprised. Maria and her mother stopped crying. They looked at Oweka in amazement, not knowing what he was after. After he had finished hurling the things, he turned to Maria.

"Can you get out of here!" He was pointing to the door as if to tell Maria the road to follow. Maria stared in unbelief. How could her father treat her so? "It seems I am talking to someone deaf. Let me get my panga." He dashed out and Maria's mother started crying. "Oh my daughter run, run, run for your life, run, run ..." Her half-brothers joined her mother. She realised that there was no hope. Oweka was not joking and he would never change his mind. She jumped out through the window and walked sluggishly for a few metres, then stopped. The boys also left the room.

Oweka entered panting. "Where is she, where is this fool? Where ..." He did not see anybody else apart from his wife. "What are you doing here? Can't you follow your daughter?"

She did not hesitate. Oweka was worse than a lion if he lost his temper. She got out and went to Maria. When Maria saw her mother, she felt a pang she could not describe. She saw nothing to remain for. The world she wanted was full of hatred. "What else can I do apart from leaving this home?" she asked herself." I have to leave here. I have to leave my mother because she can't go with me. If she wants to leave, let her find when and where. I will have to go alone and face my fate alone. I hurry to my doom alone. My mother has nothing to do with that. I go to my end alone. I go." She started to leave the compound.

"Maria, where are you going? Come back," her mother pleaded, "where are you going? Maria, come back. Come back!" Her words came out generously but instead of soothing Maria, they heightened her feelings, her anger. She answered her mother hysterically.

"I am going away mother. You don't want me any more. You have chased me. I am going to suffer because it's my fault not yours. You don't deserve any suffering, mother." With this last word she turned her back on her home. She hated Oweka, she hated her home and never wanted to call it her home any more. She slipped in among the bushes. Nothing on earth would make her go back to where she was not wanted. The moon had disappeared. She made for Jimmy's house, the cold morning breeze blowing against her, thoughts in her mind, troubles in her heart. Whether for worse or for better, she would see.

CHAPTER FOUR

Jimmy was half asleep, half awake. He seemed to he struggling with something. He was dreaming. Something, most likely, a lion, was chasing Maria. She had wings but when she tried to fly, her wings could not unfold. There was a big tree nearby and she decided to climb it but it suddenly became so slippery that she resorted to running. All the same, she could not make any progress. She was just jumping around on the same spot. There was a bus standing nearby. Somebody from behind her advised her to jump on it. When she made to jump, the bus left and Maria remained desperate.

He woke up all of a sudden. Something seemed to be wrong but he could not tell what. He lay waiting, then there was a loud knock on the door. He frowned. What Jimmy had hated since his childhood were people who knocked on doors in the early morning. He was determined to frustrate the person knocking. Then it came again. This time louder. He got out of bed and pulled his trousers on. He was still buttoning when another knock came, almost breaking the door this time. It was loud, harsh and impatient. The early-comer might be the bringer of good luck, he thought while hurrying towards the door. He opened it and was stunned.

"Maria!" he yelled. Maria started crying violently. Her dress was dirty and her arm had dry blood on it. Jimmy saw the cut on her arm. "Maria, what has gone wrong? I left you in good condition. What has deformed you within this short time? What has cut your arm?"

All along, Maria had not noticed the cut on her arm. When Jimmy asked her, she glanced at her arm and she almost went crazy. The cut started hurting. She felt as though her arm was going to fall off her body. She collapsed in the doorway. Jimmy dragged her in and laid her on the bed. He was panicking. He hurried back and closed the door carefully, he rushed to the room and assumed a position by her side holding her tight in his arms. They remained in this position for some time, Jimmy trying to build up what had happened to Maria after he had left her, but he could not come to a clear conclusion. Could it be that some people had invaded her room when she was away? But then the immediate help could have been got from her people not me. Perhaps something fell on her, maybe the window cut her. But then, this is not enough to bring her back to me. Or else her people discovered. But how? I saw her safe. Everything was very fine when I left her. Jimmy wanted to ask Maria what had gone wrong, but he knew she was unable to answer him. Tension was building up in him and he thought he would burst. He withdrew his arms from her and she turned round with pain and placed his hands back around her.

"Daddy," she called out faintly.

"Yes, Maria." She did not reply. "Maria I thought you called my name? Maria, Maria." He shook her. She opened her eyes slowly and closed them again. "Maria tell me what. Please talk". She shook her head. Jimmy was puzzled. Was she dying? He jumped out of the bed. Maria stretched out her arm and pulled him back. He was almost crying when he talked to her, "Maria talk to me, you are sending me crazy. Tell me, what has gone wrong? Tell me."

Maria told him the story, breaking down at some parts and Jimmy was patient. She narrated with care, making sure she did not miss anything that had happened. She finished, and felt some relief inside. It was as if she had transferred her load on to another shoulder.

Jimmy sighed heavily and for a while his head remained blank. Then little by little his mind started working. So she has come to me, he thought. A sign of resting all her burdens on my shoulders. So things have turned to this? Just within this short moment! He turned and looked at Maria, she had no look of peace at all. She was playing with her fingers and one could see that she was completely desperate.

"Did your father tell you to come to me or you decided it on your own?" Jimmy asked at long last. It was the first time he had spoken since Maria told him what had become of her.

"No. He did not tell me to come here in particular but he told me to go back where I had spent my night which is here. Or am I mistaken?"

"Don't be harsh Maria. He told you he never wanted to see you home again and he was serious?" It was as if he was informing Maria but she understood it as a question.

"Yes!"

"What then do you want me to do now?" The question was very plain but Maria found it too hard to answer. She had come to him and surely he knew what she wanted him to do? She started crying. Jimmy realised the mess he had made. He lifted her, laid her on his chest and started rocking her. Her tears dropped on his skin. The tears were warm. He loved her, but now he hated the situation in which he loved her.

"Maria, listen to me. Please understand me. Don't cry. When you cry you almost send me crazy and you complicate things. Tears have never been a solution to problems, instead you are wearing out your heart. You are a big girl now. If you could control your emotions, we would try to work out things together. Use reason not feelings! Let's work our heads together instead of sacrificing tears that will never provoke God's mercy. Do you get me?" She nodded her head and wiped her tears. Jimmy pushed her head gently away from his chest. She started shivering. "Are you feeling cold?" She shook her head. "Why then are you shivering?"

"I just don't know. I am troubled. I don't know what will become of me."

"Don't worry, my dear, things will work out, you'll see."

"You speak as though things are easy, Jimmy. Words are easy to say, I know that, but I know things won't be easy for me. What will I do? I have no qualification. How will I go through the world, without a home? I have no parent to lean against. The way you see me is the way I am armed to fight against the forces of the world. Will it be possible Jimmy?"

"Why? Maria, why can't you trust me? I understand you, perhaps better than you can guess. I know what is existing between us now. It's a problem, but you have to understand that some problems cannot be solved overnight. We need time. Maria, with time, we shall get through. We need patience, please. You may think it's only your father's home that is your home but this too is your home. I know the rest have rejected you. You have no father, you have left behind your mother and brothers and you have no hope of having them any more, but Maria, I will be all of them to you. I will be your father, your mother, your brothers and more so, the Jimmy you have all along loved to have for ever. When I was leaving you in that fateful room didn't you say you wanted to be with me for good? Ha, ha, ha, Maria, I know the rest have rejected you but despite the fact that I am alone I am ready to fight. I will fight on your side. I am alone but I am ready to fight. I will fight on your side. I am alone but I will fight them. Forever I will be on your side."

Maria sighed. She didn't know where the words came from and she didn't know where they belonged. Whether they were a mere flattery or a real generosity. She could not tell but she felt the words go through her, laying peace in her heart. She felt loved. She felt warm under his care. There was nothing to compensate for Jimmy's love and kindness. She kissed him gently on the cheeks. Jimmy was surprised at the sudden change.

* * *

She woke up so suddenly from her sleep. It seemed something had woken her up. But where was she? It was not her room she was sleeping in. Then it came back: a few hours ago she was expelled from her own room. She was now in Jimmy's home. For how long had she slept? She picked up her watch from the table and was surprised to find that it was four in the evening. She had slept for so long. She turned her face towards the window and found that the sun was sending its rays directly on her. She immediately turned her back towards the window again. The day was already old and she felt a bit of hunger pinching her stomach. All over her she felt physical relief. Jimmy had already given her enough time and room to rest. But where had he gone? The whole house was very quiet and there was no trace of anyone outside. It seemed to her he had left many hours ago.

She became uncomfortable with the window open and got up to close it. She discovered a chit under the table with her names printed on it. It could have been blown there by the wind. She opened it and found in it instructions for her. Jimmy had written to tell her where to get all the necessities. Above all he encouraged her not to lose heart. It was normal to have problems. "Try to find something to eat. I am by your side. Don't mind because I didn't tell you goodbye, I kissed you in your sleep." Maria smiled at these words and she stretched herself in readiness to find something to eat. Then she felt a pricking pain in her arm. The pain went direct into her brain and she went breathless, she fell back on the bed, and remained in it for some time. She got up, warmed some water, dissolved salt in it and then started washing her wound. The pain was now increasing so she decided to go and sleep. After all, she was not terribly struck by hunger. The pain was sapping her energy.

Back in bed, she felt bored. She tried to find something to keep her occupied. She got Jimmy's photo album and turned its pages slowly but nothing was interesting. She had seen them again and again and knew them almost like the palm of her hand. Jimmy and business friends, social friends, drinking, debating, his early days at school... She could tell what was on the next page before she opened it. It was boring and she dropped it. She looked around and there was nothing else to entertain her in the room apart from the radio. She would have sat by the TV but that meant moving to the sitting room yet she wanted to lie on the bed. She stretched her arm and put the music on. Unlike the early days, today she found big mistakes in every song. Some were dull, some almost sent her crying, some made her catch nostalgia.

She turned the music off, lay on her back and her mind started wandering, "What is going to happen to me? Will I get out of this deep pit? Sometimes I see myself smartly through. Then I will go back home reconciled to my people. But will father accept reconciliation? If he will not accept me easily then I will remain close to others and give him time to consider. There is nothing else I will be able to do.

"What if it turns out that Jimmy gets married to me?" She took a deep breath. "Will I manage that kind of life? Get up early, make breakfast for him, cook his lunch and supper, produce children for him, wash his clothes, manage all his other domestic affairs and the list will go on! Then what in the end will I get for doing that? Will he be a good man and tell me 'I have got a woman in you'? Then I will feel loved. Or will he turn out to be unkind? After trying my best he will instead quarrel and shout at me for being a dependent under his roof?" Tears crowded her eyes. She decided to think of something else. She could not however find that something else to think about. Her mind whirled around Jimmy and herself.

'Yeah! Today I am in Jimmy's house, yesterday I was in my father's. What about tomorrow, who will offer me a life under his roof? How could all this come to happen? How did it happen? How did Jimmy come into my life to give me problems?

She could still remember everything. It was when she was going back to school for her second term in Senior Six. Oweka had insisted on her arriving at the bus stage early, so she left. Her brothers escorted her up to the bus stage and left her there. They promised to come back and check on her after some time but they never turned up. She understood. Oweka could have distributed tasks to them and they had to finish them before sunset. That was how Oweka was. After her brothers had left her she felt so bored but there were some people who were also waiting for the same bus and it seemed they were in good company because they kept on laughing. Maria moved close to them. They were innocent men from the innocent countryside who talked what they were innocent about.

"The countryside is more interesting, "they said. "Booze is very cheap. You can get dead drunk with just a coin." One man talked of how he visited his daughter in the city and felt pity at the amount of food they ate there. "Everything here is easy to come by except money, but after all we have the things that we would have needed money for."

Then they started mocking women. "Women are difficult to understand. It seems they even don't travel. It's as if they don't have what to do outside their homes once in a while. Just wait and prove it today. There will be about sixty passengers in the bus but women may number up to five only. Women, women ..."

There were some women around and they tried to defend themselves but they could not win. "You men are always up and down. Where will we throw the children if we also started your ways."

"That's not the reason, "the men refused.

"But some of you force us to live within the home, what else can we do?" They all laughed. Maria was amused but she did not show it. Then they went back to talking about what had brought them to the stage. It seemed the bus was not coming. It seemed all of them had some very urgent business. It would be today or they would fail. They kept quiet in sadness. Even Maria felt impatient. It was getting late and she might arrive past the set time. She didn't want to be punished.

As if in answer to their prayers, they heard something like a vehicle approaching. They all got excited and some of them started lifting their luggage nearer. Then a small vehicle appeared. They frowned in disappointment and hurled dirty words at the vehicle. The vehicle pulled up and everybody knew its driver, including Maria.

"You are still waiting for the bus?" he asked.

"Yes," they answered in chorus. Maria discovered that they loved him and liked talking to him. She knew that most people respected him because of his wealth. It was discussed in the villages that he changed vehicles like a woman and knickers. They all knew him as Uncle Jimmy. Despite his wealth, he was a very jolly man. He never set social limits.

He too was doubting the arrival of the bus. "The bus might not come. It could be in the garage, it's an old one you know." Maria felt like crying. "But never mind it could come. I am not saying it will not come I am just doubting." He talked to everyone and at least had something to amuse all of them. He knew all their names.

After he had amused them, he proceeded to Maria. She was surprised to hear him call her by her names, because she thought he didn't know her. Maria could not hide it and even Jimmy noticed that he had surprised her. He helped the situation.

"Are you surprised I have called you by name?" he asked and before he could finish Maria had already replied.

"No!" it came out strongly.

"But you seemed to be surprised."

"I just seem but I am not."

Jimmy laughed. "So you are going back to school today?"

"Yes"

"Ha! I wonder whether your bus is coming ..."

"Is it really my personal property?"

Jimmy ignored the question and proceeded. "This government should give us two buses on this road. One bus is not efficient at all. At times, it breaks down, at times it comes very late and passengers suffer, appointments fall..." Maria did not believe in the reality. All along she had thought Uncle Jimmy a very proud man, hard to approach and therefore she feared him. She had always hated meeting him. He greeted her whenever they met but she thought it mockery. Yet today he was here, speaking to her as if they had been friends for a long time. It was not difficult to get used to him. She now felt as though he was a mere equal not a parent. But what puzzled her was how he came to know her by name.

"I wish it would come," Maria spoke into the silence.

"What?"

"I wish the bus would come."

"Are you worried? Do you want so much to see school today?"

"I am worried because we are expected on the school campus today. If I don't fulfil that then I will have to undergo a punishment which I don't like at all. I am praying the bus comes. I can go even though very late."

"Ha! Then you are in shit. No, but you can do the punishment. There is no way out. This bus is not coming as far as I know." Maria got hurt. This man is funny, she thought. Instead of helping me to pray he is telling me something else.

"It's not a simple punishment and it may not be only a punishment."

"You are sure you really want to go?"

"If I could even fly!" Maria was looking troubled.

"I could help you if you don't mind. I know the problems of being a student, I was once one. I am travelling past your school and even if the bus turns up you could save that money. A bus fare can be very expensive, for a student. Let me see if I can be of good help."

He left unceremoniously without bothering to know whether Maria was ready to acknowledge his offer. He got into his car and drove off. Maria felt so thankful and developed some love for Jimmy, thinking I wish everyone was as concerned and loving as this one. Deep inside her, another thing puzzled her. So he already knows my school. It seems he has been investigating me. She brushed the thought away. It was nothing to her, her problem was to get to school.

He reappeared after ten minutes and pulled up at the same point. He got out of the vehicle and he looked different. He had changed to travelling wear and Maria liked the look of him. He approached and was playing with a bunch of keys in his right hand.

"I am going to help the student. You people can wait for the bus. If it does not come, make sure you don't die tonight." Everyone laughed.

"Yes, you help the student. Those people are still under strong control. With us, we can decide never to go where we want and nobody will be there to ask why," an arrogant young man said. His words had encouraged Maria to travel with Jimmy and instilled more fear in her that the bus might not come. He offered to carry Maria's luggage on the back seat and they sat in front.

"Keep on waiting, I am only taking the student," he announced and drove off. They drove about thirty minutes in silence. Maria had already started feeling uneasy. She wanted him to talk. Then he cleared his voice, hummed a little bit of a tune, then glanced at Maria and smiled.

"Do you like music Maria?"

"I love it."

"That's better. So you'll be going back to dance. Do you like dancing?"

"Yeah, but I can easily do without it."

"How do you like your studies?"

"I like it, I like it very much."

"That's very encouraging. I remember when I was still a student I loved my studies so much but when I remained with only a few months to go, I felt school was hot. I wanted to do away with it."

"Everybody has that feeling."

"Is it?" Maria did not answer. Jimmy glanced at her for the second time. "How is Daddy?"

So he knows my home too and my people. "He is fine," Maria replied and turned her eyes away.

"He must be a proud man. I mean being proud of you. It's not an easy thing to educate a child." Maria did not comment. "So what kind of woman do you want to be? What do you want to do in future?"

"It will depend on my passing. I have to read hard of course."

"Yeah, you are very right. Do you want to get married in future? I know most girls at your stage take marriage to be a filthy affair. Do you take it so?"

Why all these questions? Maria thought. She wanted to change the topic but she could not. Then she replied, "I will consider marriage when it comes but, for now, I have never thought of it. I may marry, I may not."

Jimmy laughed briefly. "You could be very right Maria. See a man like me, I think I started thinking about getting a wife immediately I got out of my mother's womb..." Maria laughed. Jimmy seemed touched, at least he had amused her. "Yes, it sounds funny but it's true. I always thought of nothing other than a wife but up to now, I have never had one."

Maria was surprised. "Surely you have no wife?"

"It's a pity Maria."

"Why are you not married?"

"I expected the question. See, most people think a man who lives up to this age without a woman has something bad about him. He could be a drunkard, greedy, a womaniser. Yes, and the list goes on, you can add yours, Maria. I have never been any of that. It's women, women have been a big problem to me."

"How have they been a problem?"

"Sorry to speak ill of women before a woman. Pardon me if I have hurt you, Maria. Generally speaking, I have failed to get a reasonable woman under the sun. You get this one, she cheats you, another one is quarrelsome, the other wants to be the man in the house."

"Why do you blame all women? Why don't you talk about the ones you have come across? It seems you like generalising things."

"Maria, your words encourage me. I have never given up hope, I still believe there could be a good little wife somewhere. I still have big hope, I will never give up. I have a feeling of love, love for someone I don't know but I know I will soon get hold of her."

"How have women been a problem to you?"

"I thought I told you. The rest are my problems alone, not yours, and I believe in secrecy when it comes to personal affairs."

Maria kept quiet. She was already tired of his questions and bored with his bachelor business. It was not her problem if he had failed to get a reasonable woman. Exactly as he had stated. Everyone has his own shoes to pinch him but she kept on wondering why he talked about women as if he had completely resigned from them. Maria was happy to be quiet but Jimmy started again before they had gone far.

"School is very interesting and it's the best time in life. When you come out into the world, you long to go back to school."

"You must have had a very interesting life in school."

"It was not interesting but at that time I didn't care. I simply did things without bothering. I had the spirit. All students are like that." Maria didn't respond and he continued, "I was a very stubborn boy at school. My mind always planned mischief. There was a time I wanted to punish the Headmaster. I ambushed him and threw posho crumbs at him. It was at night and he could not discover me. The next day in the assembly he cursed, and swore to expel the students if he discovered them. He did not, because I planned it alone, did it alone, and never let it out to anyone. Later on I was expelled from the same school. I fought a teacher. We used to line up for food and I thought the exercise degrading. I would just head straight and get my food. This teacher thought I was being proud so he got my plate and broke it. I lifted that teacher and pushed him into a huge pan." Maria giggled.

"I joined another school, a mixed school this time. There I got involved in an affair with some girl. It was unfortunate for us, she got pregnant by me. I was however lucky that some teachers were also after the same girl. I influenced her and told her not to betray me. She accepted to lie that it was one of the teachers but I promised her secretly that I would marry her. I won the case and I still remember how the girl's parents cried. Her mother almost killed herself with rage, 'How can I send my daughter to school to be taught by you teachers and you are the very ones to ruin her?' I did not however marry her. She misbehaved. I thought about my son with her but I could not claim him because I had denied responsibility. Sometimes I feel guilty about it. I made that girl suffer, bringing up a child without any source of income. Anyway, God forgive me.

"The teachers in that school hated me so much that I failed to progress any more. I joined another school again. From there, I managed to go through without much trouble. I took care because my father swore to fix me hard if I misbehaved again. I joined a teaching course and came out as a teacher. Then politics came for us: I quit teaching and joined it but quit politics too when it landed me into trouble. My political rival sent me behind bars. I joined business after great years of frustration. Perhaps one day I will quit business too but for now I like it. You cheat and you are cheated. A very democratic game indeed. See, I still dream of politics but one thing I will never quit is searching for a wife. It's becoming too late and I am getting worried about not having a son."

He told Maria much about himself and Maria kept on wondering why he was behaving so. He drove her up to school and left her without ceremony. He did not even wait for Maria to finish saying thank you. "He is very complicated," she thought. "Sometimes he behaves proudly, sometimes sociably, sometimes kindly. He is a chameleon." She told her friends about it and they had mixed feelings. Some warned her and said he was simply playing monkey tricks on her: that was the way they all started, by being kind and parental and when you think you are dealing with a parent, you realise he has become a husband when it's too late. Others brushed it off as just nonsense to say he had something hidden. He was an understanding, kind man. He'd known Maria would get punished and he had to help. That is a big man and experienced, so if he meant something, he would have suggested it there and then. Such a man can't beat about the bush like "colonial boys". They laughed and agreed that it was fun for Maria. Two weeks later, Jimmy sent Maria a card. The card had music and Maria and her friends ran mad with excitement. It was wonderful to them. Those who had suspected Jimmy now confirmed their suspicion.

Even Maria realised what Jimmy was after and she cursed herself for accepting his lift. "This is a very funny man. He is not married, he is looking for a wife and he thinks he will get one in me." Maria swore he would never get her. "He will try just like any other man but he will obviously fail."

However those who were against it continued talking behind Maria's back. "Maria is pretending. How can a man give you a lift just for free?" they would question. "She must be in love with him."

"In love with him? No. I cannot believe it, it's a lie."

"Yes, most girls can do it. Merely because the man maybe has money. This one who brought her seems to be the kind. He even has a car."

"I cannot fall for such an old man because he is rich. I would rather come to school naked if my parents can't afford a dress for me rather than do that. That is ruining oneself."

"It's up to her."

"No, we have to get concerned. Old men have never been good to girls. It's hard to become friends with them."

"Why do you care when she seems to be comfortable with him?"

"It's up to her, then." They would always give up the gossip with "It's up to her."

It was now the last Saturday of the month and this was a visiting day in Maria's school. For Maria, that was the day she hated so much. No one came to visit her on these days and she felt desperate when she saw her friends being hugged and loved by family members. Maria had asked her father to visit her but he refused saying it was too costly to travel. She could not convince him. To avoid envy, Maria decided to take her books and go to a lonely place. But she could not read. She turned the pages of her books and prayed that the time would pass. Then one of the prefects came to call her because her uncle had come to visit her. Maria's heart leaped. She could not believe her ears. How could an uncle come to visit her? It was obviously bad news. She started wondering who was dead. She hurried and was surprised to find Jimmy waiting for her.

He smiled at Maria but she did not respond to his uncle. Why did he pass himself off as an uncle? She wanted to turn back but thought it unwise, so she approached.

"You are welcome."

"Thank you! Are you surprised to find it's me?"

"I am very surprised." Maria turned round to make sure her friends were not listening to their conversation, but they were already getting suspicious. Maria had never told them about any uncle. Her uncles, she said, were poor. Where did the car-owning one come from? Jimmy took her to his car and handed her a bag, filled with gifts. He had given her another surprise. It was hard for Maria to reject the bag in public so she took it. In the dormitory she unpacked many gifts arranged in a decorative way. Her friends really admired her. She said that he was a family friend and her father had sent him to her.

"Your father surely loves you," they exclaimed.

She returned the bag and had a little chat with him before he drove off. He did not tell her anything like love. She was grateful for the things but inside her she was afraid. Jimmy was laying a neat trap for her, she was getting into it at a slow pace and there might be no hope of escape.

He always took her by surprise and in a place where it was hard to protest. She feared creating a scene. "No, there is still time," she thought, "one day I will get an opportune moment and I will break through the trap. I will take it as fun and when he suggests more, I will reject it. I will tell him that I thought he was helping me as a parent." Jimmy became her constant visitor and each time he came, he increased the value of the gifts. Maria found herself liking everything and she found herself sometimes sitting by the gate with other eager girls. When it seemed Jimmy would not turn up, she felt a fever and her tears would hang within. He would turn up and Maria would get excited like a puppy that has seen its master. Jimmy ignored her emotions and always left Maria without any word to make her feel better. She hated this. She now wanted him to change the way he talked to her, she wanted him to be a bit sentimental and she felt a pinch of jealousy when Jimmy showed concern for her friends.

At the end of the term, Jimmy drove to Maria's school and offered to take her home. Maria was so excited and she accepted willingly. Jimmy looked moody and behaved to Maria like a real father. He advised Maria to read hard and avoid men. Men are not good. Maria felt so ashamed. Why did she mistrust Jimmy? He was being a father and helpful. Maria felt like running away from her real life, but she could not. There was another feeling of frustration. Jimmy had drawn her and her heart had followed. Why was her heart so cheap? She hated Jimmy. When they had driven half-way Jimmy stopped at a trading centre and took Maria to a cheap bar and lodging. He ordered all the drinks Maria wanted and went outside.

"Keep my daughter and serve her all she needs. I am going for business and will be back in a while," he told the waiter. Maria drank quietly, feeling embarrassed at the way she had misunderstood Jimmy. It was the waiter who made her talk whenever he asked her what she wanted, otherwise for the rest of the time she was quiet and felt the drinks entering her head. Jimmy spent a long time away and Maria started feeling impatient. It was becoming late and he had many apologies for Maria.

"You see people here are not punctual enough. I had to wait for them for hours. I am afraid we have a problem." Maria's heart leaped. "I don't know what we shall do. The car is down." Maria was about to cry but Jimmy was fast enough. "The condition is not bad. It will obviously be repaired. Some men are already working on it. I am only worried that we shall reach home late. Don't worry, just trust me. In case the car fails completely, I will find you a place to sleep. You'll not suffer, you are a young girl and you don't deserve suffering. I brought you all the way from school and I am responsible." He suggested a walk while the car was being worked on but Maria turned it down.

"What if I met someone I know, what would I say? How can I explain what I am doing here?

"You can find a reason. You are with a parent, you are with a friend, what else?"

"No." They decided to sit and drink but they talked less. Maria was so worried about being away from home on such dubious grounds. Then Jimmy went out and came back smiling.

"Yeah, I told you the car would be well. We can go now. Oh, we are saved from the trouble of sleeping away from home." Maria jumped up but collapsed back on the chair. Jimmy lifted her with his left hand and paid the waiter with his right, then tenderly guided Maria to the car.

"So she was drunk." He smiled and drove off at a very slow speed.

They had covered most of the distance and home was only about three miles further on. Jimmy pulled up. It was now dark.

"What is wrong?" Maria asked.

"Just something about the car."

"Is it down again?"

"Not so down. I can put it right. Give me a torch, it's just in the bag at your feet." Maria got it and gave it to him. "You can get your head in here and see it. You may drive one day and you'll not be knowing such simple mistakes in the car. Maria moved closer and her head was by the steering wheel, just near his. He turned the torch off and grabbed Maria's head, he turned her lips towards his and kissed her. Maria was too surprised. She had never been kissed before and here today she was being kissed. Why was he doing it? What was wrong?

"Maria," Jimmy whispered.

"Yes?" She was trembling.

"Did you know I loved you?"

"No".

"You mean all along you had not seen it in me?"

"No," she lied.

"There is the truth then. Have I surprised you?"

"Yes."

"It seems everything about me is surprising to you?" Maria stayed quiet. "Maria I love you. I have been taking this long trying to find a way and today is here. I have got you. You are the woman. I love you."

"I am sorry I thought we were just being friends."

"Of course, lovers have got to be friends, Maria. I am not forcing you. You have to think about it. I have just laid it before you to consider. Please, take your time, I will be patient." He held her to his chest. "Maria kiss me, too, will you not kiss me? Be kind. Come on."

She didn't know what to do and this filled her with rage. She didn't know where she got the courage from but at least she surprised him a little.

"I don't love you. Leave me alone. I am sorry, I didn't know these were your motives. Please leave me alone. If it's for your car, I am going to foot it to my father's home." She made to open the door but Jimmy pulled her back, ignored her venom and went on talking. His words coming out like a cool breeze, he shattered her efforts.

"Maria, it's not any crime for you to kiss me. Kiss me, don't be shy. Come on, Maria, come on." She started crying and shivering. Jimmy kissed her. Then he bit her ear, she felt blood rush down her legs and she coiled. "Maria, I love you." She kept quiet. "Please understand me. Do you believe I love you?" She pulled his head back. He laughed. "Maria, answer me, do you believe I love you?"

"Yes." She lowered her head on his chest and he kissed her hair. She withdrew from his chest.

"It's very nice for you to believe I love you. Now, do you love me too in return?" Maria's heart was long decided but fear ran within her and before Jimmy she felt weak and could not speak her mind.

"Maria, be quick. I am dead with emotions. Do you love me?" Still she didn't answer. He lifted her onto his lap and her head was almost touching the roof of the car. "Maria, I know you love me but you just want to torture me. Maria ease me. Say you love me. Just say yes. Maria say you love, say it, let me hear it from your mouth, say it..."

"I love you," she replied amidst tears. Jimmy got excited like a little child. He kissed her and she thought he was going to swallow her. The sweetness of being loved was overwhelming. Oh, it was sweet to love and to be loved. "Maria, I love you too, I love you too. You are mine and I am yours. You'll take me and I will take you. Have me, take me, I am yours."

CHAPTER FIVE

That day, Maria reached home very late and her father was cross about it. He warned her about travelling at night. "The night is not safe. Couldn't you sleep at school and come tomorrow if you were dismissed late? These teachers also want to put our children into trouble. How do they dismiss the students so late and yet some have a long way to go! What did you use for coming? The bus had already come."

"I used my friend's father's car," Maria said.

"Did he make you pay?"

"No."

"What a good man!"

He doesn't know, Maria thought. During that holiday Jimmy took her out twice. On the first occasion, she told her father he was going back to school for a seminar. Oweka did not hesitate and he gave her the money. She entered the bus and got out just at the next centre. She found Jimmy waiting for her and they drove off to a very beautiful big town. There, they entered a big, beautiful hotel. Jimmy suggested they should go straight into their room and be served in there. Maria did not hesitate and Jimmy was happy at the way she was becoming lively and romantic. In the room, they found magazines. Jimmy ordered drinks but Maria did not touch any, she only ate and read almost all the magazines. Jimmy was drunk and said he would sleep early.

That night Maria did not sleep, she was too scared of sharing a bed with Jimmy. She quickly discovered that he was not asleep. He touched Maria, kissed her and fumbled with her dress. Maria jumped out of bed and sat on a chair. Jimmy got up and carried her back to the bed. He wanted her so much but she refused. She was resolved to remain clean throughout the affair.

"Jimmy, let's just sleep"

"Maria!" Then he forced her to lie on the bed, covered her with the blanket and he also followed her under it. She decided to turn over and she wound the blanket round her. Jimmy tried to disentangle her from it but he failed. He was drunk and weak. So he lost. The next day in the morning he was so moody. He refused to take Maria in his car and gave her money for the bus. She did not care as long as she kept on winning.

He did not give up. Next time, he took her back to the bar and lodging he had first taken her to when he brought her home for the holidays. Jimmy took her to a room and held her urgently. That day she was lucky, she had her period. He looked like crying and she pretended to be concerned.

"Jimmy, has it disappointed you?"

"Maria you are bad."

"It's not me Jimmy. I cannot help it." Inside her she was mocking him and feeling happy with nature.

It seemed Jimmy gave up. He did not try anything again. The last term began and he kept on paying her generous visits. Maria thought him so good. He was really a good man. A man who doesn't say I don't love you any more because you have refused to offer a night is really a real man. Then after her exams Jimmy invited her to his home.

"You must be tired from books. Come and let me relax your mind a bit. This time it's not going to be in a hotel, it's going to be in my hut." Maria told her father that she was going to the trading centre to buy something and she would delay a bit. "I may come back in the evening," she told him. Oweka was displeased by her intention to come back in the evening, but he reluctantly let her go without asking why she would have to delay.

It was going to be the first time she entered Jimmy's house and she was eager about it. The house as she approached it was so ugly, a small thing, almost a hut, with dirty walls. But when she entered it she was astounded by the luxury. It was beautifully furnished. It stood as a symbol of wealth. There were easy chairs, beautiful pictures hanging on the walls and the carpet on the floor added to the general beauty. Everything inside was organised with care.

Jimmy invited her to sit on a large easy chair.

"Please sit here."

She sat with her mind resting on the beauty. Jimmy realised it but he let her continue. Maria had, before this, thought her father was wealthy but Jimmy's wealth disqualified her father's. Then she remembered what the economics students used to tell them. That in economics, growth was not development. Her father had grown but he had not developed. In science, they knew that growth was development but in economics

70

growth was growth and development was development. Books can really twist things. She smiled at her thought. Jimmy was all along looking at her.

"What is amusing you?"

"My thoughts."

"Are you comfortable?"

"Yes."

"Good." Jimmy went back and locked the door. "I don't want people to disturb me. When they see the door open they will know I am in." He went to a cupboard and brought a bottle of beer. Maria drank alone and he smoked. Maria became dizzy and Jimmy moved close to her. He squeezed her fingers and she closed her eyes in pain. Then he softened, then he squeezed again. Maria had a vague memory of the rest. Her head was turning round, then he laid her on the sofa. She remembered feeling him remove her clothes. He kissed her all over. Her head continued turning round. The whole world was dark and then she felt a pain. It continued and she cried for mercy but he did not have any pity for her. Then he finished and started kissing her again. Her lips were dry from crying and she felt them crack. But it wasn't that! She moaned and he comforted her.

"Don't cry, I am through, it won't kill. Oh Maria I love you." She did not answer. Then he got up and told her to dress. When she was getting up she saw a patch of blood on the sofa. Maria fell back and started crying. Jimmy carried her and started dressing her. He finished and held her on his lap and started rocking her.

"Maria, it's not anything bad. It's normal. You won't feel any pain again. It's like that with every woman. You are very nice, Maria. Thank you for it!"

She burst out. "I don't want... Don't say thank you. I did not offer anything to you. You tricked me into it. How can you rush me into things?"

"You mean I have been rushy? Maria, I have been patient for eight months now, I have not rushed you."

"No! You have rushed me into things. You are bad, you are bad..."

"Will you forgive me for that?"

"I will not, you are bad, you are a liar."

"Maria, don't call me names, don't blame Daddy. I did it because I

71

love you. Maria, I don't lie, I only love. That's the best way to say I love. It speaks, Maria. It speaks more than words. It's louder. I didn't mean to hurt you. We have to do if we love each other. Don't blame me." She could not blame him any more. She was sitting on his lap, he was very many years older than her and he was talking to her like a father and his little daughter. She respected him instead of loving him.

"Maria, you seem to have understood me, have you forgiven me?"

"Yes, Jimmy."

"Call me Daddy, not Jimmy."

"Why?"

"It's sweeter."

She knew he would still bug her if she didn't say it, so she accepted. "I forgive you Daddy."

"You are becoming nicer every moment."

It was hard to begin with but after this incident they both went crazy about love. They over-did it. That was what had landed Maria in this situation. She turned on her stomach, closed her eyes and tried to sleep but she could not. She had not eaten. It was already dark in the night and Jimmy was not yet back. Could be he was so busy. She started sobbing.

* * *

As soon as Maria had gone to sleep Jimmy wrote a note for her and slipped out of his house. He did not do business anywhere that day, he just drove his car to a lodge and demanded a room. He wanted to rest from Maria's tears. Perhaps away from her he could do something instead of comforting her. He spent almost twenty-four hours in the room but slept little and he was unaware he had wasted so much time. His head was heavy and he could not think clearly. Thoughts kept on coming and before he could reason one out, another came in. He felt his heart weighed down with trouble and he saw his real happiness slip away.

Jimmy had great experience with women and it was not any task for him to handle them. Some needed a fist, some crocodile tears, some bent knees and raised hands... He knew them all but this one was really hard. "Things don't seem well with this one," he said aloud. She was a mere student and she wanted to rest all her burdens on his shoulders. Above all, he had lied to her, a very big lie and he didn't know how to handle it. How would he hit the truth without sending her crazy? How was she going to live with the truth? Things were impossible. Why did he lie? But he had to lie and the lie wasn't a great mistake. He had to succeed by lying. The lie wasn't the mistake. They had lost control. And now they had got an accident. He sighed. "I thought I would be careful," he thought, "and I knew I was being careful but then I wonder what the hell has done this. I thought things would remain as sweet as ever."

He remembered the time he first saw Maria. He had thought there were no more extra-charming girls under heaven! He swore never to let her go. He was resolved to strive hard. Yeah, the pink dress she was wearing was simple but her beauty made the dress great. She was gentle in her all. He could not hold back. He asked the man he was with where Maria was from and he told him everything about Maria, loading it with praise. During holidays, he would frequent the trading centre with the hope of getting Maria, but she was not easy to come by. He would go to church pretending to pray but looking for Maria. Unfortunately she was always in the company of Oweka and her mother.

He dreamt about her, her shape in a pink dress kept on haunting him. He was almost going crazy about her, when that day he got her. God was surely for him and made the bus break down. At last he got the stepping stone. He was so eager to tell her his mind but he realised she was hard and he would end up failing. He decided to be slow and sure. Sometimes behaving honestly, sometimes hiding himself in the guise of a parent, until he got her. He succeeded but the next step was hard. She frustrated him until he almost gave up. However, he swore to give up only after a great struggle. Then he retreated until she thought he had given up.

He was planning the best way to trap her. He hatched it and fixed a day. Everything was indeed planned and he invited her for the first time to his small house. Then he started feeding her on beers until she was completely drunk. Her head was heavy and her eyes rolled. He touched her and she responded. Her brain had gone down the drain. Beer had done it! She was thinking just between her thighs. He guessed his time had come and he guessed right. He moved close to her and held her in his arms, she in turn put her arms around his neck. Then he withdrew his hands, she was too weak and she collapsed on the sofa pulling him down with her. She lay on her back and he was just over her. He decided to try her. He kindly asked her whether he should kiss her and she faintly accepted.

Blood rushed to his head and he went blind. He kissed her as though he wanted to put the whole of her in his mouth like a sweet. Then he touched her all over. She protested but her voice was faint and welcoming. He undressed her and she did not care. Then he kissed her again and again till she became willing. He held her hand, then alone he started groping for the gate; her weak protest made his way hard. He made it at last. She screamed but he could not tell whether it was in excitement or in pain. For him it was a wonderful tour.

He held her and moved with her, together they toured the island. Oh, what a beauty to live in it. He wished it was his home for ever. It was unexplored, nobody knew the secrets behind it and its beauty. He was the first to reach the island. He had made a discovery. It was like a dream. Then he developed wings.

At the end of it all they discovered that they did not have wings after all. So they had not gone anywhere.

He looked at Maria and she was weeping, her eyes were red. He tried to comfort her by kissing her. She moaned, so he pulled away and looked her in the face. He saw her lips were dry and he felt sorry he had hurt her. She got up and just under her was a patch of blood. He had hurt her there, too. He felt guilty. Then she started cursing and blaming him for going against her will but he managed her and she was soon quiet. At last he had succeeded in winning her.

This incident. Oh I wish it had never happened, Jimmy thought. The incident was like the beginning of the slope. They were carts being pushed down the slope. They could not control anything. They rolled until they reached the bottom. Yeah, it's true: they lost control, they let their emotions lead them to hell. Even Maria became romantic; a day without being together would never happen. She surprised him by her sudden change. He had fun with her and she took him back to days when he was still twenty. He lived in her heart and he prayed to God to condemn death. Above all, he swore to take care but instead things had turned against him.

He now had Maria to deal with. How was he going to manage? He turned and sighed. The good times were over, perhaps they would come again, this could just be a mere rest from it. He remembered the times he had with Maria. After he had tricked her into things she never hesitated again whenever he wanted her. He had all he wanted from her. She even followed him without invitation, to his house.

One day, he still remembered so well, he had invited her to his house. It turned out that he became moody. He had some problem, he could not remember so well. He had no heart to talk so he decided to give her what would entertain her, music, beer etc. and he retired to his seat. Maria kept on disturbing him and she did not give him time to think.

"Jimmy, why are you moody today?"

"I am not moody, I am only thinking."

"What is that?"

"It's my problem alone, don't mind."

"But I want to share it with you."

"No, you can't do anything."

"I will just stand by your side while you fight."

"Take it easy, Maria."

"Then you don't love me."

"Oh I do, Maria." She got up from her chair and sat on the edge of Jimmy's. Jimmy moved a little for her, then she proceeded to play with him. She pulled his hair, she bit his ears, licked his neck and he felt good. A number started playing. It was not a famous one but Maria loved it for its words.

Baby I am tired
Tired of waiting
Waiting for you.
You are my lover
You are my angel tonight...

She kissed Jimmy's neck gently and whispered, "Jimmy, I wish you were the one who played that number." He was surprised.

"Why? Why?"

"Oh, I would not at any moment doubt your love. I would love you, whether in heaven or hell. I would not leave you even if the divine powers tried to intervene. I would surely feel proud."

"Maria, up to this moment you don't believe I love you. That man has the words but I have the love. I am not talented with words but I

75

would really make you feel the weight of my love for you. If you can weigh it, you will be surprised. Never mind, Maria, after all I identify with that man's words."

"You say you don't have words to express yourself - where did you get all that from?"

"Yes, those are the words I can bring out, but are they as big as the love I have? Maria, tell me."

"Jimmy."

"Yes, Maria."

"Don't you think music is great?" She wanted to change the topic.

"Yes, music is great. Very great indeed."

"How great is it to you?"

"It makes me happy."

"Yeah, it makes everybody who likes it happy. To me, I feel great. I wish I were given the honour of giving awards to inventors, I would honour the one of music most. I wonder how it came into his mind. Could be a 'her'. That is the greatest inventor, isn't it Jimmy?"

"Maria, you think like a witch."

"Oh, how I wish I was a witch, I would do this. I would become very small and enter your pocket. Then when you are carrying on your business, you could want to pick something from your pocket, maybe a pen, you would see me instead, as little as a bean but smiling as ever. You could leave me in the pocket and smile, then your mates would think you a jolly man. Then from inside here, I would become big and offer you all my love. Don't you think it would be very great?"

"Yeah, it would be great, but it can't happen."

"I can make it happen."

"Oh, you frighten me, Maria. I told you, you are a witch."

"Yes, I can make it happen."

"How?"

"I will love you and haunt your mind."

"You will kill me, Maria."

"No, I will love you." He turned and kissed her and they rolled down on the floor.

Jimmy was lost in his thought, then he realised he was not with Maria, he was in a lodge and all the good had passed. He turned and tried to sleep but his thoughts had aroused him and he felt like holding Maria again. He wanted her again. What would lying away from her do? It would only add to their loneliness. He jumped out of bed, opened the door and hurried through the corridor. He asked the watchman to open the gate and explained. "I have a business far off and I have to begin my journey now so as to reach early enough!" The watchman looked at him with suspicion and hesitantly opened the gate for him. Jimmy drove off and soon forgot the watchman. He wanted to reach Maria as soon as he could.

* * *

Maria opened the door and Jimmy was there, standing. He looked worn out, his clothes were creased, his hair was uncombed and, as if for the first time, Maria realised his age. She made way for him and he stepped in. Maria went back to her position at the door, the east was already getting clear and the birds shouted everywhere. They seemed happy. She locked the door, then turned to go to the room. Jimmy was standing at the centre of the sitting room. Maria ignored him and went to the bedroom. He followed her then. He sat on the edge of the bed, put his hands together and remained in that position for sometime. He sighed and started planning what to say.

"Maria," he said, his voice low and tired. "I am sorry, I left here yesterday, when you were sleeping. I left a chit here, informing you where to get everything. Did you get it?"

"I got it."

"You got it. Yet I can see that nothing has been touched except this bed I am seated on. Why? You mean to say you still don't want to eat? Are you not hungry?"

"I am hungry."

"Now, why can't you get something to eat?"

"I could have. But my arm."

"Oh, I had forgotten that. So you want me to get you something to eat? Do you want it?" He did not wait for her answer. He started pumping the stove and soon water was boiling. He buttered some bread and made tea. They were both hungry but they ate little. Jimmy had not lost the spirit of talking.

"Maria, did you get bored being here alone?"

"Not so bored. I slept most of the time and I thought a little."

"What was in your mind? What did you think?"

"I had some thoughts. I cannot describe them so well."

"You are lying."

"So you know what is in my mind better than I do?"

"Yes, I know better. I saw you thinking most of the time and sleeping little. You thought I had left you. You thought I had run away from you and you cursed after me and sacrificed your tears for the gods of the earth so that they could destroy the tyres of my car and you made me come back home very late. Maria you are bad. Why did you make your gods destroy the tyres of my car? I will pray to the very gods and they will destroy your shoes." Maria smiled. Jimmy noticed it. "Good," he added but Maria did not know why he said good so she ignored it. He proceeded with his talk.

"Maria, let's get serious now. I know, Maria, you were worried. You must have thought I was gone. Well, I am sorry for staying away from you for all that long. It's the kind of work I do. It's not a good job to be a businessman. You have to sacrifice everything to get profit, otherwise you flop. When I left here, I thought I would be back soon. Unfortunately I was unlucky. The first thing was that my car broke down. This car is becoming rubbish. I should dump it. Remember last time when we first entered the other bar and lodging. Oh it was a nice time. Those are days to remember, but we still have days to make. Sorry. Yeah, I got into another vehicle then I had to bring a mechanic to put it right. I started doing everything late, therefore. I wanted to come here immediately I got over with my work but my friends refused. They said it was risky to travel at night. I had to stay but my heart was here. Immediately the first bird whistled I left without a bath, without breakfast."

"Is that why you are shabby?"

"Yeah, you can prove it from the way I look."

"It's better for you to get yourself smart, someone might call in and find you in that state."

"I am in my house and I am going to make sure no one comes in. I am going to leave that door locked. Who will force me out?"

"Why do you want to remain indoors?"

"They are not greater than you. I am going to talk to you. I want to talk to you. Maria, we are here, so close to each other physically but I don't think we know each other so well. Maria, we don't know each other and yet we are beginning to live together." Maria was so surprised, she did not know what to contribute. He continued. "Apart from knowing me as a businessman, a man who is your lover and then a small bit of my school life, I don't think you know more than that. I told you I am not married. That does not mean that I did not have any woman to love at all. I have tried many women, Maria. The first woman I was seriously involved with was that girl I told you about. I did not tell you how she disappointed me. In other words, she did not disappoint me, but I disappointed her, I am sorry, Maria, to tell you that. You know, Maria, when I was with the girl, I thought she was the real woman to marry. She was a beauty, surely, but when I moved out of that school I started meeting other girls who were greater than her. Coupled with the fact that after conceiving she went back to the village and got rotten there. I never wanted her any more and I was ashamed of her. I was really very lucky that she had accepted that it was the teacher who was the father of the child. So when she came to me I told her boldly that she was confused. 'How could two men be the father of one child? At first you declared before everyone that it was the teacher, today you come to me that I am responsible. Clear off!' She went away crying. She had refused the teacher thinking I would take her."

"That's how you ruin them?"

"Maria, it's not ruining. Well, it may be ruining but it's not my intention. Put yourself in such a position. You loved a boy when you were still in Senior Four and promised to marry him. Then it turns out that you beat him in education. You come to the village and instead of finding that boy you loved in Senior Four, you get an old, dirty man, with stinking clothes. Will you really love him again?"

"Well, it depends..."

"On what?"

"On what caused it. Take for example, if he relaxed and drank while I studied, I don't think I would sympathise with him. But if my love made him so crazy that perhaps he got expelled from school and he suffered as a result, I become responsible instantly and though I will not marry him I can still help him in one way or another. I would not throw him off as you did."

"Maria, you are talking because you have never been put into such a situation. You are talking out of ignorance and innocence. If you were in that situation, you might be surprised to find yourself doing exactly what I did."

"Well!"

"Whatever it means, I am sorry if that story has hurt you, Maria, but you should know me. We should not be strangers. Perhaps another thing that made me do that was age. I was young and I never felt pity at all. Now when I tell the story, I feel pity for the poor girl. She is now a woman, anyway. Well, this incident taught me a very big lesson and, though I loved girls, I took care. I did not get so committed. Then after my course, I thought of marrying. There was a woman already. I took her but she turned out to be a beast. I never got anything from her that I had expected."

"What had you expected and how was she a beast?"

"There are very many things a man wants in a woman. I think she was not taught by her mother. She did not respect me in any way. She was all the time arguing over simple things. She asked me questions all the time and wanted to know me down to my toes. I got tired. She game me nausea..." Maria laughed. "It's true, so I had to push her off. I tried many more but I got none. I therefore decided on a game of play and leave until I got you. It's unfortunate that before we walk any steps ahead, this happens and now you are here with me, forced by your parents. Well, that does not matter. There is only one thing I am driving at, Maria. I involved myself with all those women and of course some did not leave me barehanded. They left me sons and daughters. Keep it therefore in mind that I have a family, though incomplete because I still lack a wife."

"And where are they?"

"Well, this is not my home, I live in it, alright, but it's not what I can call a home. My home is not here, you know. I told you this, didn't I?" Maria didn't answer. She was not sure whether he had really told her. He proceeded. "That is one thing to consider. Another thing is my work. I don't need to tell you much about it, Maria. You are a learned woman and I think you know what business is. I will have to travel and I may be away from home for many days. You will have to understand that. I don't want to come from my work and then find you here boiling hot and cursing me for involving myself with other women. I used to do that but I know I am a changed man. I will therefore want an understanding woman." Maria had nothing to say. She could not commit herself by saying she could be understanding. She was also wondering why he was telling her all this. Was it important to her in any way?

Jimmy started speaking again, as if he had read Maria's mind. "You may be wondering why I am telling you this, Maria, but I want understanding. If I don't tell you this today, someone may tell you tomorrow and then you will hate me for leaving you in darkness. You will think me an unjust man and then you will begin cursing. You will think I was using you. I don't want that misconception, Maria."

"I don't mind that..."

"Exactly! That is exactly what I wanted in you. In a woman," Jimmy rushed in before Maria could proceed.

"I don't mind that," Maria started again, "What I mind so much is what you will do for me in future, keeping in mind that I am a student."

"That's not anything difficult, Maria. That is a very easy thing. The way we shall be tomorrow will depend upon the way we organise ourselves today. I know you are eager to discus that but let's give it time as we look around. Time gives us better answers and so we shall wait. I am by your side otherwise."

It was nice for Maria to feel unrejected. Jimmy had surely understood her and kept her warm under his roof. In her heart, she promised to do Jimmy all the good she could as an appreciation for the understanding he had. She relaxed her mind and started playing with him, caressing him. He had told her his past, a sign of love and commitment. Why then should she think about her father's home? Where she is already an outcast. Where they don't have a grain of love for her, where she was tortured and turned away. Down with them! Jimmy was here to love, so generous, so warm and fine. She wanted her people but they didn't want her. What else could she do?

"I am not to blame," she said aloud.

Jimmy overheard her. "What's that?"

"I am not to blame."

"For what?"

"For leaving my family. I wanted them but they refused me the right to live with them. I could not do anything. I tried tears but it did not plead for me. What else could I do apart from walking away? Who will blame me for walking away? I have a right to find love for myself. I have the right to walk where there is love, to find love. No one can deny me that. I don't say I am all in the right. I know I went wrong but no one accepted I was repentant. Perhaps if it was God he would have forgiven me. But this was Oweka, my earthly father. He was no god so he did not forgive me. What else can I do?"

"Yeah, Maria, you are right. There is a time you really want the world to understand but it will deliberately refuse. What can you do in such a situation? You really try but they are hard, and there is no hope. You give up, Maria. There is nothing else you can do. Why fight a war you are sure you will never win? Your future however is not sad, Maria." He lay down near her. "I am here for you. When they beat you, you come for comfort here. When they reject you, I will open my door wide for you. When they call you names, I call you my darling. When they say they hate you, I will say I love you. I will offer you all the comfort. I will be your all."

"Jimmy, thank you for being kind. You are loving and I will hold you, I will love you. Jimmy you are great." She buried her face under his arm and started sobbing. Her tears went through his shirt and onto his chest. He held her and she held him too. They loved each other. Before them they saw none other than them. What if Oweka had sent her away? An act of an ignorant parent. They were two and they were enough for each other. Why had they wanted other people? Why did Maria cry for her father? Jimmy loved her more than him. He had got her. She had got him and they were content.

"I have got you, Jimmy," Maria whispered.

"You are the woman, Maria."

It was three in the afternoon when they woke up. Jimmy was feeling hot and dirty. He looked too old, perhaps eighty years old. He felt a bit of rest inside him. Maria felt dull. Since she left Oweka's home, she had not taken a bath.

"We have slept so much, Maria."

"I feel relief inside me."

"It has done us good. I feel like I am meeting you for the first time. It's as if we have nothing to disturb us. I feel very hot and dirty. I think I should bathe."

"I would like to bathe too. I last took a bath on Easter day."

"Get the water then and let's have a bath."

"My arm."

"Oh, sorry." Jimmy carried the water and they bathed together.

They played with the water, laughed together and spent more than thirty minutes bathing. They felt fresh and hungry. Jimmy sent Maria to cook. She was busy and happy and kept smiling over her work. It was just hours but Oweka was already becoming remote to her. She thought, "I will stay patient until he suggests reconciliation. I don't need to worry, I am safe and happy here." She served the food and they devoured it like hungry lions. After eating, they had nothing else to do so they resumed sleeping.

CHAPTER SIX

Life became a stream of honey to Maria. She spent a whole day without thinking about Oweka or her mother. At first Jimmy tried to keep everything secret but his very walls let out what he was hiding. It all started by whispers and then murmurs, whistles, alarms, then drums came in; everything was out.

Oweka now knew the man who had ruined his daughter. He sent threats to Jimmy. "Tell that man I will teach him how to be content with his wife alone."

Jimmy would report it to Maria: "Your father says he is coming to teach me how to be content with my wife. I wish he would come. He would be surprised to find out that I am really so content with my wife, his daughter." Maria would laugh. Days dragged by and Oweka presented no real danger to Jimmy, until his threats were like a dog barking from an opposite valley.

Maria and Jimmy became open, they had nothing to hide now. They were always seen together, walking hand in hand. Sometimes he taught her driving. When Jimmy was away on business Maria would be busy getting things ready for him. He would always come back to find a surprise for him. Sometimes he got flowers in the pocket of his coat, sometimes small exciting gifts he could not describe. Maria was really a woman.

People started admiring her again. She was a young girl, much younger than Jimmy, but she was making a very good wife for him. "Jimmy should surely marry her," they prayed. "She is really born lucky. Maria is lucky! After her father turned her out of his home we all thought she would perish there and then. But see, she is sprouting. It's hard to know God's ways. Once he has loved you, you'll never shed tears."

Maria's mother sometimes slipped out of Oweka's home and visited her. She would tell Maria about all the fresh developments. At first Oweka remained so bitter, he did not listen to anyone. Simeon tried in vain to convince him to pardon Maria. He did not talk to anyone. Every day, he added to the store of his clubs in readiness to kill Maria if she appeared. When news reached him that it was Jimmy who had ruined his daughter, he wept. It was sad. He knew Jimmy. He was far older than Maria. Why did he ruin his friend's daughter? Oweka did not eat for days. When he recovered, he swore to kill Jimmy. But he had no energy to do it. He would also deal with anyone who visited Maria. "No one can go and visit my daughter under such a roof. Oh Jimmy!" he cried. He started considering whether to forgive his daughter. However, the venom still infected him.

"Maria, you know that all this is your fault," her mother said. "You have to be as patient as possible. Maybe your father will forgive you, maybe not. If not, then your fate is already clear. You have to live with this man. I will try to be by your side. Your father I know is not happy about your relationship with Jimmy. That may be to our advantage. Don't ruin yourself. He may be just about to call you back. However, next time, you'll have to take this as a very good lesson. If you don't change your behaviour I may die."

"I will not ruin myself mother. I will wait for father to forgive me," Maria would assure her mother. However, when she was alone, she almost laughed at her mother. She had never wanted to lose her parents and brothers for good but she would not die to regain them. She had all she wanted under Jimmy's roof. Nothing was really there to push her.

"Maria, I am happy you still want to come back to us. I will pray to the Lord that he changes your father's mind. I always plead with him. I no longer fear anything about him. He at times slaps me, abuses me, says I disturb him with silly things. To me it's not silly, you are my daughter, my only child. I want you back and I will never give up pleading with your father." Maria almost cried with pity for her mother. She had known through her step mother what suffering was in Oweka's hands. She was lucky Jimmy was there. She had escaped Oweka's wrath by running to him.

"My child, listen to this. When your father takes you back, don't turn to this man any more. This man is not good. He is too many years older than you. You are still a very young girl, you could even be his daughter. You will get better men as you get on."

"Mother, I stay with this man because I have nowhere else to go, otherwise I would have left him. I am regretting all I did."

"I am happy you are getting to know this. Maria, listen to me, don't disappoint me. You know how I suffered because of you, since you were a child. I would have long ago left Oweka's home, but because of you I suffered. And now, if you disappoint me, you'll have mocked my suffering. Listen to me as your mother."

She was very tragic in her ways. Maria felt for her but from inside her, she knew leaving Jimmy was going to be hard. She loved him, she liked him and she never wanted to leave him. On the other hand she wanted to comfort her mother. She knew very well her mother had no one besides her and that is why she would slip out to find love. What could she do? She wanted her mother. She loved Jimmy. Maria would try hard to resolve the conflict and instead end up crying.

Jimmy would appear like a saviour. "What, what's that? Crying for daddy? Oh Maria, keep quiet, come on, I am here. Why are you crying?"

"I missed you," she would lie.

"Sorry for keeping you bored. Oh work, work, I wish I could avoid it, I would have you all the time." He would hold her and roll with her on the floor and within only minutes Maria would have forgotten her mother's plight and the desire to live forever with Jimmy would get stronger.

He would at times drive her out for evenings. One day he drove her out to a big hotel. Oh, Maria marvelled, everything looked wonderful. It seemed to her everyone here knew Jimmy. He talked to all of them and they laughed together with him. Maria looked at them with keen interest and Jimmy felt pride big in his heart.

"Do you know all of them?"

"Yes," he would reply, then look at Maria and smile. They gave Maria huge handshakes and she felt great being recognised. His friends offered her drinks. It was late in the night and they had not yet left. Maria suggested they should go.

"No!" Jimmy refused. "Maria, we are not going back home. We have stayed there for days without change. I am tired of it. It gives me nausea. Let's have a change tonight. Let's sleep here. Do you mind?"

"I don't mind but you should have told me earlier on."

"It would have been no surprise. I wanted to surprise you."

"Thank you."

"Do you feel sleepy now?"

"Yes."

"You suggest we go to sleep?"

"Yes."

He got up and Maria followed. The room was well decorated and very bright, Jimmy sat on the bed and summoned Maria to follow. "We can sleep straight off."

Maria was soon under the blanket and she was about to fall asleep. Jimmy turned off the light and followed her.

"Maria, are you feeling so sleepy?"

"Yes."

"Can't you find another word, you keep on telling me yes!"

"Yes."

Jimmy laughed aloud. "Don't sleep, I want to talk to you about something"

"We can discuss anything tomorrow, I am tired."

"No it's now, it's important, we have to talk about it here or never."

Maria's heart leaped and she was soon sober. "We can get over it."

"Did I shock you?"

"No."

"Good! Maria, well, sorry to start unceremoniously but this is something I want to tell you. We have lived together now for some time. It's not so big a time but I call it great. This is what I want from you. I want a child. OK?"

"Is that why you stopped me from sleeping?"

"What do you want me to tell you?"

"Jimmy, you are not serious." Maria was feeling hot inside her stomach.

"I am very serious. I want a child from you. Why don't you want?"

"Jimmy, I am still a student. I am staying with you because my parents have rejected me. I have not come to you because I want to be a wife. I am not ready for a child, I have to read. How will I read with a child?"

"I will look after that. What I want is a child!"

"Jimmy, I am not going to heed that. You are the very one who told me you would take care and my parents would not know anything. You ran crazy and came between me and my father. Before you can help me out of the problem you want to dig another pit for me. You will never force me to have a child I don't want."

"Are you quarrelling with me?"

"I am explaining. Jimmy you have to understand. You don't need to think about yourself and forget about me."

"I don't need to argue so much. We shall see that later on, we shall see." He turned and slept. Maria did not sleep any more. She prayed for her father to forgive her before it was too late.

87

The next day they drove back home quietly. Jimmy opened the door and picked up a letter which had been pushed in under the door. He opened it, read it and sighed. He sat on a chair and covered his face. Maria sat near him.

"Daddy, what is wrong? Is it sad news?" He handed the letter over to Maria. She read it. Somebody who called herself mummy had come in but was unlucky to find no one. She has expecting Jimmy home the next day without fail.

"What is it Jimmy? Who is she? Is she your mother?"

Jimmy sighed and his face relaxed all of a sudden. "Yes."

"What could be wrong with her? Is she sick?"

"I just cannot tell. I cannot tell what. I have to get there now."

"Can I go with you! I could be of help if she is sick."

"That's not your concern, you will stay here." He jumped up, went to his car and drove off without ceremony. Maria was left in suspense. She did not know exactly what was wrong. She felt like crying. She felt like following him but she didn't know his home village exactly. She decided to hold her heart firm. Jimmy did not come back that day. Maria turned over and over in bed until she felt her skin irritated. The next day, the sun set again and Jimmy was not to be seen. In the night Maria kept on expecting him. She closed her eyes then blocked her ears, expecting Jimmy the next minute, but the world remained quiet. No one knocked. She felt desperate.

It was now a week. Thoughts started flocking into her mind. Has Jimmy deserted me? He must have used the letter as a stepping stone. She wanted to leave but for where? She could have cried but Maria had now learnt that tears could offer no help.

It was the morning of the nineth day since Jimmy left. Maria had given up hope. She had two things to do, to leave for somewhere else or to wait for her death in Jimmy's room. The latter was the probable one. She had nowhere else to go so she decided to wait for her death. She lay quietly with uncoordinated thoughts in her mind but all lingering around one thing, her future. Then she heard a violent knock on the door. It was obviously Jimmy's. She got up and opened the door.

"How are you Maria?"

"Welcome back Jimmy. You left without ceremony and you almost disappeared for good."

"I was worried about you, of course."

"Were you really worried?" He went into the house and sat on a chair. "Daddy, what went wrong with you there?"

"Oh, I got a hell of problems to settle. I knew you were dying this way but I had nothing else to do. You will forgive me."

"What was it?"

"Too much, Maria. I am too busy in the head. I will tell you that later on. It's only that I have been left broke. I am not staying here for long. I have to look for money. I just came to inform you."

"So you are off in no seconds?"

"I am off."

"Some tea, something to eat Daddy"

"It will delay me. I am OK." He stood up to go.

"Daddy, you are going surely?"

"Yes. Is there anything you want to tell me?"

"There is nothing great to tell you. Safe journey, see you."

"OK. Bye." He made to leave, then Maria remembered she had no money.

"Excuse me, Daddy."

"What is it?"

"I have no money and I am running short of everything, for how long will you stay away?"

"I am not very sure. It will depend on how much work I will get there. Anyway I will try to do things very fast and get back soon. Right now I have not a cent with me but you could try to economise with whatever you have. I will see you soon."

Maria said nothing and he drove off. She went back to the house and resumed sleeping. Her mother had stopped frequenting her. Oweka had discovered where she had been going and tightened his rules against her so it was hard for Maria's mother to leave home. Maria therefore remained lonely most of the time.

Jimmy came back after three days. He was moody and refused to talk to Maria.

"Didn't anyone come here asking for me?"

"No one. What is troubling you, Daddy?"

"How many times do you want me to tell you that you are not concerned?" Maria left the room and sat outside. Jimmy called her back immediately.

"Maria, why have you left me here alone?"

"I wanted to give you peace."

"Did I tell you I was troubled? Are you the one to give me peace?" Maria kept quiet. He smiled, but a dry smile, and proceeded to talk. "Maria, I need food terribly, I am too hungry. Can you get me something to eat."

"I have run short of everything."

"You mean you have been starving?" She didn't reply. "Oh, I am very sorry. Go out and buy food." He offered her money and she left. He started working out ways of approaching her. He wanted to talk to her but he didn't know how. There was a loophole in every approach he tried. He decided to postpone the talk. Maria brought him the food but he refused to eat.

"Jimmy, were you serious you wanted food?"

"I wanted it at that time but you've delayed with your cooking. You can eat it, I no longer want it. You say you have been starving since I left, isn't it?"

She moved the food and went back to sit outside. She admired the trees, she looked at the birds and beyond them at the clouds. They looked peaceful and she wished she was part of them. She was puzzled in her heart. What had gone wrong with Jimmy? Was his mother dead? But can't he tell her? Maybe he is tired of me? He must be planning a way to get rid of me. Maybe I have annoyed Jimmy? But this is a big man, can't he tell me where I am wrong?' Maria's mind wandered in the wilderness and it could never find a place to settle. She buried her face between her knees and started working out what to do. She decided to go and approach him. He was lying bare-chested on the bed. She sat near him, silent.

"You have decided to come back?"

Maria ignored the question and brought in hers. "Daddy, what makes you so moody with me?"

"Maria, if you can't sleep then you better leave me alone."

"You may think you are behaving in a great way but you are torturing me." He turned his face against the wall. "Daddy, you mean you don't want to talk to me?" Maria insisted, hoping to win him, "Daddy, please, are you not going to talk to me?"

Then he shouted, taking Maria by surprise. "Maria, get out of there if you cannot keep quiet. Don't bother me!"

That night Maria slept in the sitting room. She felt cold but she feared being close to Jimmy. He would perhaps beat her. She got up very early in the morning and warmed herself under the morning sun. He also got up and followed her.

"Good morning, Maria."

"Good morning."

"Can you tell me where you slept last night? I am sure it was not in my house here. You were not there beside me."

"I slept in the sitting room."

"Why?"

"You told me to get out..."

"If you could not shut up that is. I did not tell you to go out to other men. You slept somewhere and I want you to tell me where you went. Was it your aim to follow me here to cheat on me?" Maria failed to talk. She was too surprised. Was Jimmy going crazy? "You can refuse to talk to me Maria, but I will know the truth, and immediately I get to know it, know you are done with." He went back to the house immediately. Maria followed him into the house. He was combing his hair.

"I am going to check on my friend. I will come back for breakfast." He dressed and left. Maria prepared the breakfast but Jimmy did not come back. He had gone on foot and where would he be? Maria was bewildered.

That day, her mother came to see her. Maria was so excited that she almost collapsed. Her mother didn't stay for long because she feared Oweka would discover her absence.

"Maria are you worried? What is disturbing you? You don't look like before."

"I am a bit worried, Mama. I don't know whether I will pass. And if I pass, will I be able to resume school? Is Daddy talking about getting me back?"

"Sometimes he talks of it but sometimes he talks against it. You know your father is very hard to deal with. But I know it will come one day with the influence of his friends. I am also pushing him."

"Mother try hard. I want to get back home. I don't like staying here."

"Is he mishandling you?"

"No, I just want to get out of here. Home is better."

"I am glad you are after that. Let's be patient and put it in prayer.

91

God will help us one day." She left and Maria remained lonely.

Jimmy came back at midnight. He was drunk and staggering. "Maria, where is my breakfast? It's supper time but I want breakfast. I remember before I left here I told you to make me breakfast." She warmed it and served him. He ate everything and went to bed. Maria was planning to sleep on the chairs again but he called her.

"Maria, why do you hate me?"

"I don't hate you."

"You hate me. You cry when you see me and you don't want to sleep in my bed any more, why?" Maria had no answer. "And you are growing old and ugly. Why? Get up and let me see your shape." Maria could not help laughing. Jimmy was perhaps acting and not really being serious. "You can laugh but you puzzle me. You hate me and I cannot tell why."

"How did you come to think I hate you?"

"So you don't hate me?"

"I don't hate you. How can I show you I don't hate you, yet you don't stay with me here?"

"And that is exactly what is making you moody. You imagine I am cheating on you. I cannot find a better way to explain this to you. If you could only remember, in the beginning, I told you I would be on and off. Maria, we have to come to an understanding otherwise you will break your heart over nothing. At times I am moody because, I told you, I have problems. Domestic problems. I cannot tell you them now but I will tell you later. Understand me. I am broke now but if I get money I will not leave you to suffer. I love you and I cannot rejoice in your suffering. He pulled Maria onto the bed. "Maria, let's have a child. Let's have our child and we shall be three. You'll get company when I am away instead of being dull in the bed throughout the week."

"Daddy, I am not ready for that, I told you. If you want a child, then be patient and let me get through with my books. I am not ready now."

"What if I die tomorrow?"

"And you leave me with a child. My parents are not by my side, who will care for the child? I am not ready to suffer like that girl you told me about."

"That's the reason why you are denying me a child? You think I will turn you off afterwards, but I told you that I am now a changed man."

"That is good but it is no reason."

"Well, we don't need to argue but we shall soon get one."

"Jimmy, you have to understand." She started sobbing. Jimmy held her and started caressing her.

He stayed with Maria for four days and Maria felt life getting back into her. Then he left again and promised to come back after three days. He left her with just enough money for three days. He stayed away for two weeks. Without money, Maria tried to manage but she could not afford good meals and most of the time she had black tea. Then the sugar got finished but she still had the tea until that, too ,got finished and she started starving. She waited for Jimmy but he did not appear. Maria's fears were confirmed. Jimmy was trying to get her out of his house. She longed for her father to take her back but she waited in vain. If she had had somewhere else to go she would have left Jimmy. It became too much for Maria. She was obviously going to die if she was not going to find food. Her mother did not appear. She went to the neighbours and asked for help. They gave her food and they spread her suffering to the winds.

Jimmy came back again. He was sorry about everything and promised Maria he would not leave her. He went for work, and came back, sometimes very late, sometimes very drunk and he became a burden to Maria. She wished him gone. He blamed Maria for everything bad. He shouted at her and Maria felt like a child. He resorted to quarrelling with her almost every night and in the morning he apologised and blamed the beer for it.

"Maria," he would say, "You don't love me, you love my money. Your father did not send you away from home. You just hatched a plan to come here because you thought that here you would belong to my great property, my wealth. I don't believe your father sent you away. I took you to your room and I left you safe. You tell me your father was hiding in the room; so why could he not get me, too? He would have even got me and left you. You only wanted to come here but I am sorry you have done it the wrong way."

Things started disappearing from the house. When Maria asked Jimmy, he told her they were his property, why should she ask? Maria developed a hatred for Jimmy but she had no one to turn to. She told him she loved him but inside her she knew that, if she had a dagger, Jimmy would be her first victim. She endured it because she wanted to get back to school and only Jimmy could help her. At times he would not speak throughout the day. Sometimes he would disappear and when he reappeared he had no apologetic words for Maria.

"I thought I would find you gone."

"Where do you expect me to go?"

"Anywhere. I thought you would get bored and go."

One day, Jimmy came back early from work. He had courage inside him, courage to tell her he had lied. That the truth was this. He had failed all along to do it but today he was going to. The only thing was to approach her, in whatever way, and whatever effect it might bring. The only thing was to approach her. He called her to the room.

"We have stayed for long without talking. I want us to talk." She sat next to him and remained quiet. He had expected her to talk but now that she remained quiet, Jimmy felt uneasy. The courage he had left him. How was he going to start?

"Get me some drinking water." She got it for him and resumed her place and remained silent. Jimmy closed his eyes. His inner self was encouraging him but when he thought of it, his heart leaped. He would try anyway.

"Maria." She raised her head and looked at him. "Why can't you talk?"

"I don't feel like it."

"Then you should develop a liking. It's silly for us to live like dumb people. It makes inside here cold and I become a coward." She smiled carelessly. He noticed it. "Well, that is good, though not excellent."

"What is good?"

"Very good! Very good!" He laughed aloud and clapped his hands.

Maria was surprised. Why was he behaving like that, like a young boy? He may be going crazy. Who knows, with her as a burden. She might be too heavy for him.

"Jimmy, are you mad?"

"Very good! Here with your silence was hell. Now we can talk. I am sure we are going to talk. We are going to take matters seriously. You know, Maria, where we have drifted, we should find somewhere to cling."

"Well?"

"We should look this problem in the face. I can see we are trying to ignore it and yet time is rushing. We shall soon be caught unprepared.

94

Let's not try to pretend we are OK. When we do that we are postponing problems and when we postpone them they multiply, see that?"

"What should be done then?"

"A very good question! Good indeed. What should be done with what we have now? You know, Maria, that you are a student, you have fallen out of favour with your parents, you have come to me because I contributed much to your problem, what exactly do you want me to do for you?"

Maria kept her peace. What exactly had she wanted? The question lingered in her mind but she could not find the right answer. What exactly had she wanted?

He waited for her answer but it did not come. He realised he had put her in a confused state. He decided to help her: "Maria, this problem needs great thinking and you should not leave me to think alone. When you keep quiet, you make things too hard. If then I may ask you: you are a student, what do you want me to do? Do you agree to marry me? Is your coming here a sign that I should marry you?"

"I am a student. I can't get married, I need to go to school. I should get over with my education, Daddy. I can't get married now."

"So you don't want to get married?"

"No."

"You no longer love me because I am the man who made you get into trouble with your parents?"

"Marriage can come afterwards."

"But how will it be? How will you live together with me and we be able to pretend we are not lovers? How will it be for that long period, until you finish school? Then it would be better if you stayed out of here."

"Where do you want me to go?"

"I cannot decide exactly. Don't you have some relatives? You could stay with them. An aunt, uncle, anyone can do." Maria sighed. Oweka's brothers and sisters were mere memories. Her mother's brothers were worn out with trouble. If her mother could not go to them, how much less could she?

"Maria, I am not merely refusing to shelter you. I have one problem which I am sorry I did not tell you about. You will be Christian and forgive me for lying. You will sincerely forgive me. Maria... Maria,

95

I am married. I have a wife who will not agree to living together with you. I want to protect you from her. Remember when we went to the hotel and slept there then came back and found a chit? She was the one. I took you to the hotel because I wanted to protect you. I knew she was coming. The problem is she has heard about you and she has gone crazy about it. She always swears she is going to come here and kill you. Maria, I love you and I don't want to see you die. Don't you have anyone to stay with?" Maria felt the world rolling around. Sweat ran down her armpits. At last her hell was let loose. She sighed again, this time so deep.

"Why didn't you tell me that earlier on? Why did you keep on telling me you had no wife? Why? Why?" She slapped him hard but he ignored it. She felt her temper rising like a fire.

"I wanted to love you. Maria, I wanted you. If I told you, you would let me down."

Sorrow overcame her temper and she started lamenting. "I wish I knew this, I wish I had known this. God forbid! I wish I knew this, I wouldn't have. No, I would not have known you, Jimmy."

"Maria, stop being selfish. I loved you so much and you wanted to deny me it. What else could I do? I wanted you, I needed you in my life."

"You are the one who is a liar, you are selfish. You told me you had no wife because you wanted to use me and when you had led me blind me into a pit you shook off responsibility. You are a traitor. You knew you were acting falsely and you still continued to pretend you loved me. You! You followed me to put me into my grave. You ... You...!" She got up and stood before him. He pulled her to him but she resisted. "You are a son of a bitch, you are a father to bitches. God will never forgive you. You are going to hell. You are bad, you are a devil, you are hell itself. God will curse you..." Her temper was rising again and she made to strike him but he managed to pull her back.

"Maria, I am sorry if I have been all that you have mentioned. I thought I would be very careful. I tried to be very careful but fate worked against us. Maria, this is fate, fate worked against us."

"You are bad. Don't say anything about fate. You wanted to ruin me. You are a beast. I wish you could die, I wish I could kill you!"

"Maria, don't blame me when things go wrong. Don't blame Daddy."

"You are not my Daddy. You dragged me from my Daddy and you want to send me away after ruining me. You are unjust. You don't love me. You never loved me. You wanted to use me..."

"Maria, I loved you. I love you. I am not merely sending you away. I did not call you here to quarrel. I wanted us to see what we can do. I suggested that because I wanted to protect you from my wife. I know she will not like it. Well, if you have no alternative and if you feel you can bear with everything that will come, you can stay under this little roof."

Maria could not reply to Jimmy's mockery. The words "stay" from his lips sounded like vomit. She knew the words were from his lips not his heart. She could not cry. She knew Jimmy would not hold her to the last. She put her knees together and held them with her hands. Gently to and fro, she rocked herself. Love was a game of cheating and lying and for the first time, she sensed its bitter taste. She looked at the wall and it was as if she was looking through it. Before her stretched a wide, long, plain of a dark future...

* * *

Maria tried to find her way out of Jimmy's home. The only person who would help her was her mother. She was the only friend she had on earth, yet she had been cut off from her. She decided to approach a neighbour and persuade her to do so and tell her mother she wanted to see her. Her neighbour accepted and the next day Maria's mother visited her.

"What is wrong, my girl, are you sick?"

"I am not sick mother, I just wanted to hear from home. We have lived for long without exchanging messages."

"There is nothing new, my daughter. Your father is still the same. At times he gives me hope, the next moment he is frustrating me. I just don't know what I can do about it."

"Mother you mean he is still hard?"

"He seems not to be hard but I don't know what is wrong. Perhaps he is taking his time. He has a feeling that he is giving you a lesson."

"Mother, try hard to convince father. I am tired of staying away from home. Let him forgive me. Tell him I swear never to do it again. Mother, I want to come back home."

"Maria, are you suffering here?"

"No, I just want to rejoin the family."

"No, you seem to be suffering. You are no longer the same. You have grown so thin and your face is sad. Could you please tell me what's going on?"

"There is nothing mother," Maria lied. She never wanted her mother to feel sad.

"Maria, you'll not lie. I heard a bit of it. Tell me."

"It's not really that I am suffering so much. What you've heard could have just been exaggerated."

"Do you feel any changes in you?"

"What kind of changes?"

"Physical changes."

"Nothing, I am not sick Mama. It would only be that I am lonely that is why I look miserable. I only sometimes feel feverish."

"Maria, you are not safe!"

Her heart leaped. "What's that mother?"

"You are two in one."

Maria kept quiet: Jimmy had betrayed her in that too.

Her mother left and promised to come back and tell her what Oweka said. The next day she was with her daughter early in the afternoon. She had gone and asked the assistance of some elders. But Oweka could not agree. "If Maria was alone," he had said, "she could have come back but I have no room for bastards. If she can produce, she will leave that child for the man and come back here alone. She can come back later on but not now."

"We could not move him from that," she concluded.

"Mother try again. Don't give up."

"I will try, Maria, but it seems my energies will never be considered. I will try. I will try. Meanwhile you keep on praying."

CHAPTER SEVEN

Maria stayed. She had nowhere else to go. Oweka remained the same. Jimmy remained the same. He kept on insisting Maria should leave his home. He became open with Maria and did not care what he told her.

"Maria, you came here and you thought I would marry you. I have my full wedded wife and I cannot take you besides her. I have children and I cannot add you to them, that burden will become too much for me. I am a man who is always away on business. I have no time for a polygamous family. I cannot manage. That is putting myself into a pit I cannot get out of."

"Jimmy, I did not come here to get married. I don't want to marry. I simply want to go back to school and that's all. I don't care about anything provided you get me back to school."

"I will help you if I want but after that, you quit. You can find your own level in the world. You are blaming me for everything as if you were not also involved. What if I say that you made me cheat on my wife?"

"You told me you had no wife, I would otherwise not have yielded."

Jimmy would disappear without telling Maria where he was going. He left her without money and told her to her face that his money was for his family. Maria was not part of his family. Maria stayed despite his pressure on her to leave. Her mother was giving up hope. It seemed Oweka would never consent. Jimmy had removed all the property in the house apart from the bed, a couple of pots and just two chairs.

Maria was curled on the bed early one afternoon. Jimmy had not been in the house for two days. She felt the pinch of hunger but she was tired and ashamed of begging for food. They would give her the food but mock her. She no longer cared about Jimmy. His presence was a heartache to her. She had time to rest in his absence. She heard a knock at the door and she hurried to open it. Standing in the doorway was an elderly matron. Maria welcomed her with dignity but wondered who she was. She did not acknowledge Maria's welcome but just stepped in and sat on a chair like one who was very familiar with the house. Maria closed her eyes and tried to think whether she had seen the woman anywhere. She cold not remember. She gave up the effort.

"Good afternoon Madam," she greeted her. The woman replied with distaste. Maria recognised her mood and suspended the effort to try to talk to her. She sat opposite her and waited patiently for her to announce what had brought her. The woman started behaving as though she had forgotten what had brought her. She closed one eye and looked direct through the door to wherever her vision would stop. Her eye did not blink and, absently, she tapped the arm of the chair she was sitting on. Maria looked at her with apparent patience but her heart was beating at a terrible speed. Her head was functioning at speed. All of a sudden the woman came back from wherever her mind had been. She cleared her voice.

"Do you know me?"

Maria bit her finger nail and fixed the woman with her eyes, trying to place her. She could not. "No. I don't know you."

"What do you do here?" Her eyes were half-closed and she looked Maria in the eyes. Then she started rocking herself while waiting for Maria's answer. Maria started building ideas about the matron and she knew she was not far from right but she refused to admit it. How was she going to get on with her? She thought keeping quiet was the right thing to do. Then she changed her mind. It would be too rude to keep quiet. She decided to answer. It would also bridge the lull.

"I am staying here for a while."

"Since when did you become a resident here?"

"Not so long."

"With whom do you stay here?"

"With Jimmy."

"Under what status do you live together?"

Maria sighed. The questions were becoming too heavy for her. Tears rolled down her cheeks of their own accord.

"Please my girl, don't cry. I don't mean any harm. I have just come to know." She repeated her question to Maria. "Under what status do you live here?" She relaxed her face to give Maria ease.

Maria gained courage and told the woman the bones of the story from the time Jimmy met her to the time they were now seated. After she had finished, the woman sighed. They remained quiet for some time and the woman resumed. This time she talked in a parental tone.

"My dear girl," she started, "that man Jimmy is married and I am his wife." It did not surprise Maria. She had guessed it and before she introduced herself, she had already accepted it. "When I came here, I had expected to find a big woman but your age has embarrassed me. You are too young and I cannot do anything to you. I am still wondering why? Why did you agree to take such a step? That man is your father. I have children of your age. And do you know how you have made your other brothers and sisters and me in particular suffer? Jimmy changed all of a sudden. He started telling me of business. I did not get convinced, I wondered in my mind what kind of business occupied him for weeks. He became rare and I had no money to support the family. I suffered alone with the children and I am too surprised to find a young girl like you! You are my daughter's age. Have your parents refused you completely or is it you plan to stay with Jimmy? Can't you beg for forgiveness? I advise you to go back home. It's not too late. Otherwise you'll not manage. Go back to your father. I cannot take any step against you."

She left without ceremony. Maria bade farewell with another sigh. She turned her eyes in the direction the woman had taken but her eyes were filled with tears. She wiped the tears with the back of her hand but immediately she finished, her eyes filled up again. When at last she managed to control her tears, she looked to see if the woman was still there. She had gone. She sat there, motionless. Then she fell back on the chair and the woman's words started echoing back to her. "Go back home! That man is your father!! Your sisters are suffering!!!" The words became louder and louder. A cold sweat broke out all over her. The words became louder. She wanted to run away from the words. She got up and entered the bedroom. "Go back home!!!!" Maria started gathering the few things she had. She held them against her chest. "Go back home!" She stepped outside, stretched her eyes to east, west, north. Then the words "Go back home" started dying away. Reason came back to her. Was it safe to go back home? Would Oweka receive her? Her mother had told her that Oweka had gathered clubs in his house and would use them for killing her if she appeared. Would he really receive her as his daughter? Would it really happen? She turned her face to the south, she could not see because Jimmy's house blocked her eyes' way. The door opened, very wide. There was pressure on her from inside the house but its door was still open. There was no other door in the other three directions.

Maria went back to Jimmy's house again. She threw her things into a corner and lay down. It was silly to think about going back home, because Oweka would not receive her. It would never happen. Her heart was heavy. If she were to be in court and given the authority to pass judgement over Jimmy she would send him to hell at once. She was in despair and she had only herself to cling to. Her mother's energies were becoming useless. She slept.

When she woke up, Jimmy was in the house. "Why do you sleep and leave the door wide open? What if a thief enters?" Maria kept quiet and rubbed her eyes. "You can't talk today, again?"

"Your wife came here."

"Pardon."

"Your wife came here."

"My wife?"

"Yes."

"What did she want?"

"She came to tell me to leave here and go back home."

"And why are you still here?" Maria did not answer. She turned her face against the wall and jeered. She felt a bitterness inside her and something was telling her "the only way to take revenge will be to kill him". In her heart, Maria swore she would be the one to kill Jimmy.

Jimmy heard her jeer and he felt the only way to respond was to insult Maria more. "Why are you still here? I have a wife and I told you, you would never manage. I will soon want my wife in this house and you should provide room for her."

* * *

A get-together party had been organised by the prominent men in the trading centre. Couples were invited and Jimmy's invitation included Maria. Jimmy did not tell her. After all, she was not his wedded wife. He went alone. Maria saw him leave the house, very smart. He did not tell her where he was going and she did not bother to ask.

She was left bored, hungry and bitter. She had her feelings to nurse and her problems to endure. She was determined to endure to the last.

102

She sat outside and was watching the birds in the trees. A man approached. He was a familiar face, a close friend of Jimmy's. Maria knew him but she had never bothered to learn his names.

He was quick to notice Maria's mood and thought, "She might be brooding because he has denied her the fun of the party." He ignored her mood and proceeded to explain what had brought him. Jimmy had sent him for his small bag.

"Where is he?" Maria asked

"At the party."

"Which party?"

The man frowned. "I thought both of you were invited. You don't know anything about it?"

"I have known something about it from you now."

"You can give me the bag, then."

Maria hesitated. "How can I know you have been sent by him? What if you are tricking me?"

The man laughed but Maria did not join him. "You know me. I am a common man here and a friend to Jimmy. How can you begin holding such thoughts about me? I don't need to convince you but I have been sent anyway." Hesitantly, Maria went to the room to get the bag. In the room she remained standing. She was debating whether to hand over the bag.

The man waited patiently. He was wondering why Maria was moody and behaving so. Perhaps Jimmy has started mishandling the young girl, he thought. Then he started recalling the women's gossip. "It could be true," he thought. Then Maria entered with the bag. When she was handing it over to him, he realised she was avoiding his eyes and before she could turn away her tears dropped on his hands. He looked up at her. She was crying.

"What is wrong, are you sick?" She shook her head. "What then, what it wrong?" She sat on a chair and started sobbing. He was puzzled. He knelt near her and started talking. "Maria, my name is George. I am Jimmy's friend. Can you tell me what is troubling you? I could be of help."

"I want to ... to ... I want to get out of here."

"Why?" George asked. Maria continued sobbing. George thought the best way to help her compose herself was to hold her in his arms, but somehow he could not. He decided to put a question to her.

"Maria, tell me, what is wrong?" She fell silent suddenly and then started briefing him about her burdens. After she finished, George sighed. He sighed again and looked down. He thought he understood what she was undergoing. He wanted to get out of the place as fast as possible but Maria did not let him go. She felt she was still in the world with his presence. He felt touched. Tears swelled in his eyes but he controlled them. "So she is undergoing fire," he thought. He stood up to go but his conscience did not permit him. He knew very well that he was going to leave a desperate soul behind, a soul that was ready to cling to anything. He could do nothing about it. He had told her he could be of help but now he realised he was no help. His inner self however did not permit his helplessness. He kept on looking at her. Now that she was quiet, she looked more tragic. He knew what she was bearing in that silence. He found himself speaking to her.

"You could come along and have some fun with us at the party."

"I have not been invited there."

"We invited you and Jimmy, and I am inviting you again."

"I don't think you are giving me the right invitation."

"Why do you say so?"

"My presence there will not be recognised with pleasure. Jimmy did not inform me, a sign of distaste for my company."

"It's not Jimmy but the hosts who are the ones who invited you, and they are here inviting you again. Trust me, you will be safe under my invitation."

"I am not convinced. Your words don't make me feel protected."

"Besides that, I am a very close friend of Jimmy's. In case he feels bad I know how I will handle him. Trust me. I will handle the situation very well. Get up and let's go. There will be nothing bad." Without much thought, Maria agreed to go.

Half way to the party, George started regretting that he had invited Maria. He looked a fool to himself. Why did he deceive himself that he could handle the situation? If things were to turn against Maria, he would be the one to blame. Every step he took increased the feeling that he was getting nearer to danger. He had managed to convince her using a lie. He was not sure of her safety there but his legs did not draw him back. The two arrived at the party both feeling uncomfortable and each trusting in the other's protection. George maintained his strength by dwelling on the belief that Maria would be brave enough. Maria was almost dying with fear but she dwelled on George's strong assurance of protection. Neither knew the other had fear. George failed to take Maria to the open where the rest were and where Jimmy would see her. He saw clearly his stupid mistake in bringing her. He left her behind the shelter built for the party. He took the bag to Jimmy and carried back two chairs, giving Maria one. He went back for two bottles of beer, handed one to Maria and sat near her. Tension was building up inside him. Maria realised it and felt like going back. She moved.

"Don't go back," George begged her, "it will soon be dark and you will be safe." She stayed. It became dark and they moved to a position where they could see everything without being seen. Maria's eyes kept on following Jimmy. He was very busy with friends and dominated every place. She realised that wherever he passed, people laughed. Some patted him and he looked pleased. Maria wondered whether this was the real Jimmy who was a jackal in the house. He was jolly, warm and loving to all the people. He moved over to two men and whispered something in their ears. They laughed. Then he started explaining something to them. Maria now saw him clearly and he looked very drunk. The music had swallowed up his voice but from his gestures and the way his lips moved, she knew he was talking at the top of his voice.

All of a sudden, the music stopped. Jimmy's voice remained in the air, too loud and clear. Everybody turned and looked at him. When he turned round all eyes were on him. All his airs left him, he seemed to compose himself and continue talking but words failed to come out. He tried to smile, but no one smiled back.

Apparently, the embarrassment was too much and he turned to walk into the darkness. He walked towards Maria and George. He had been in the light so he found it very dark. He squeezed his eyes shut and opened them again so he could see through the darkness. He turned round and pushed his hands in the pockets. He raised his head and saw two figures seated. He approached.

"Who are these seated quietly in the darkness?" He got no answer. "Who are you? Can't you talk?"

"It's me, Jimmy."

"Who are you?"

"I am the one," he replied stubbornly. Jimmy placed the voice.

"George?"

"Yes."

"Are you the one?"

"Or I am not the one," George laughed. Jimmy joined him and felt the embarrassment slipping away. Jimmy moved nearer to them. Maria's stomach tightened. She wanted to run but George held her.

"Well, how are you George?" They clasped hands.

"I am fine."

"Why are you in darkness?" George laughed, almost a giggle and didn't reply. "Is it a silly question? Sorry, I can see you are with someone. I am sorry if I have interfered. I thought I would find no one here. I wanted to relax. I am very sorry, George."

"Take it easy, Jimmy."

He made to go. Then all of a sudden he turned back and approached George again.

"I did not greet your friend. It's bad manners. Good evening Madame." He held out his hand. Maria did not answer but just gave Jimmy her hand and remained quiet. He remained holding Maria's hand. "Who is she? I am sorry I am too inquisitive today. Who is she? How are you?"

George tried to interfere by pretending to be serious.

"Why are you so inquisitive Jimmy? Leave that hand and go back to your friends." But Jimmy continued holding the hand.

"No, excuse me. This hand seems to be familiar and I am trying to play the game of placing it. Hold on, hold on, mmm," Maria withdrew her hand forcefully.

"Maria!" She kept quiet. George started breathing hard. He wanted to run away but something held him.

"Maria!"

She decided to respond. "Yes."

"Who invited you here?" He grabbed her hand. George jumped up and started explaining to Jimmy at the same time begging for forgiveness.

"Please, Jimmy, leave the little girl. I am the one responsible. I was the one who made her come here. She had refused to come but I forced her. When you sent me for the bag was when I brought her."

"Maria, who invited you here?"

"Please, Jimmy, understand me. You can do anything you want to me but leave the little girl, I am the one to blame."

"Do you love her? Is she your woman?"

"No, she is a friend"

"Why did you bring her here?"

"I found her bored alone so I thought she would find company here."

"Maria, who invited you here?" He started twisting her arm. "Who invited you here?"

"Jimmy!" George begged.

He pushed George away and started beating Maria. He gave her several blows in the face. She screamed and collapsed. Jimmy started kicking her and she rolled over and over. George gained position and tried to hold Jimmy but he found Jimmy stronger. He lifted George and threw him on top of Maria. Others ran to find out what was wrong. They found Maria and George lying there. Jimmy was turning round as if looking for someone to kill.

"What's wrong?" they asked. George got up and explained everything. All the people blamed him. "You cannot bring someone's wife without his knowledge. He knew why he left her behind." Jimmy felt happy that he had been sided with. He went back and started drinking again. Some kind women lifted Maria and took her to her home. George followed them and he remained beside Maria for sometime after they had left.

"Maria, you will forgive me. I did not expect that when I took you there." She shook her head. Her face was swollen and her side was hurting. When she tried to talk she felt the pain so much.

"Maria, I am very sorry. I am really too sorry. I am to blame but I had good intentions." George kept on begging her for forgiveness. Each time he begged for forgiveness it seemed he needed more forgiveness. Maria wanted to explain to him that he was not to blame but she could not. Finally, she opened her lips, "Water."

George hurried and gave her water. She drank with much pain. This service to her appeased George. He felt he had been forgiven. He got up to go before Jimmy found him.

"That's the way it is George. Tell my mother to come." George left. He closed the door behind him and Maria was there alone. Then she started talking to herself like Maria was one person and she was another one. "Maria," she said, "don't worry, do not cry. You should make a tough woman. Hardened by suffering. That is the way you should be."

Inside her she was boiling hot water with hatred. Something kept on telling her. "Kill him, you have to kill him." She swore aloud that she would kill him. That appeased her. She closed her eyes and tried to sleep but the pain did not give her a chance.

Jimmy came back as it got light. He was too drunk. He just dropped into bed with his clothes and shoes on. He was soon sound asleep.

Maria got up immediately. She could not bear sleeping near Jimmy. She warmed water and started bathing her wounds. After she was through, she went and sat on the chair. She kept on looking out through the door expecting her mother to come but she did not appear. "Maybe George had forgotten to go and tell her," she thought. Could be immediately he left he shrugged off responsibility. Well, he is not to blame. Perhaps he had told her but Oweka was tight on her. Or else, she is tired of doing things that could never show any outcome. She is also not to blame. No one is to blame. George is right, my mother is right. Everyone is right apart from me. She blamed herself. I am to blame.

Jimmy woke up at noon. He was feeling lost. Then he started remembering everything that had happened. He knew everything but he didn't know where Maria was. But who opened the door for him? He remembered he got the door open. Where was Maria?

"Maria," he called aloud. She heard but she kept quiet, "Maria! Maria!" Fear ran through him. He jumped up and brushed his hair using his hands. He went into the sitting room and found Maria seated quietly. "Maria." She kept quiet and looked at him coldly. He felt guilty. "Maria why don't you want to talk to me? Don't you want me here? Do I look rubbish? Am I stinking? Then tell me to get out of here." He sat near her and started pleading. "Maria, I know all I did and I plead guilty. It was bad, Maria. I know it all, it was too bad. Forgive me, Maria. I don't know, I don't know why I did it. It must have been alcohol. I have never been like that. That has never been me. Oh dear, I deserve pity. Maria have pity on me. Forgive me. Am I forgiven?" Maria was silent. "I don't know how I should make you know that I am repentant. I don't think I have the words to use. I am really sorry and if there is anything you can tell me to do to make you believe that I am sorry I am ready to do it. Is there anything you want me to do for you?" He waited for an answer but nothing came. "Maria, when you keep quiet you make me almost crazy. People have forgiven murderers, people have forgiven traitors of their countries, why can't you forgive me? I have been repentant, I have admitted my sins against you. You are a Christian, Maria. Remember Jesus preached forgiveness. Have you forgiven me?" She did not speak. Then he got up and knelt before her. He raised his hands and started pleading: "Maria ..."

Immediately he started, Maria got up and went into the bedroom. Jimmy remained kneeling, feeling more embarrassed and guilty. Maria felt like telling him to go and kneel before his mother but she had sworn never to say even one word to him. Jimmy got up, confused. He opened the window and looked outside, then he started moving round the sitting room looking at the wall. He wanted to run away from the house but his keys were in the bedroom and he feared to face Maria. He stepped outside and stood for some minutes, then went in again. He wanted to go. He gathered courage in his chest and entered the bedroom. Maria was sitting on the floor absently. She raised her eyes, looked at Jimmy and resumed her state. Jimmy studied her for a short while. "You have refused to talk to me?" He picked up his bag and pulled bank notes out of it. He put the money on the bed. "Here, you may go to the clinic for treatment." He left the room. Maria heard him drive off. He had not brushed his teeth nor combed his hair; he had not even changed into clean clothes. She jeered after him. "I will kill you one day," she said aloud, to herself.

CHAPTER EIGHT

Two days after Jimmy had left, Maria was lying outside on a mat. She was feeling fresh from the breeze outside. Her mother had not appeared. Even George did not come back to report to her what he had done but she still expected her mother would come. She just wanted to see her. Her worries had somehow died away and she lay quiet and peaceful. A motor car pulled up. She raised her head and Jimmy was there. He opened the door and jumped out. He started waving a newspaper in the air.

"Maria, today we are approaching a turning point."

Maria stayed quiet. He must be suffering from hysteria. He over reacts to trivial things, she thought.

"Maria I am not joking, I am not mad; we have reached a turning point. Don't think I am mad."

"What turning point?"

He sat down near her, then turned to a page in the newspaper and started reading. "Listen," he said. "The Senior Six results have been released by ..."

Maria jumped up in excitement. "Oh Jimmy, don't tell me, continue." Jimmy read the whole article and looked at Maria after he had finished.

"How is it a turning point to us?"

"You don't know?"

"No!"

"I thought you wanted to go back to school. We shall decide our fate, Maria. Why do you sit here late in the evening? It's cold here, let's get inside." They entered the house. "Maria, do you think you have made it? I hope you will pass. Maria, if you pass then there will be very high hope of your getting together with your family again."

"I wish I could make it through, I can only hope."

"Yeah, I wish you could make it!"

Maria was happy Jimmy was wishing her well. He was very excited about it. He must have been waiting to see me back on track again, she thought. She felt she loved him again.

"When will you go to check on them?"

"I am not sure, Jimmy. I have just received the news you know and I have not yet thought about that."

"I suggest you go tomorrow."

"The results have just been released and I know they are not yet in the schools. I could go next week."

"No, that newspaper is of last week. I missed to buy it so I got it from a friend. I know the results are with the schools."

"Jimmy, but I fear to go and see the results on my own."

"Why? Do you want me to go?"

"Yes, you could go because those teachers will obviously discover my womb."

"That is no crime Maria. I am going to be busy tomorrow. It's not a crime to conceive. No one is going to take you to court for it."

"If you are busy tomorrow, you could go another day when you are not busy."

"Maria, you have to go tomorrow. The little money I have might be used and I may fail to get money for days. It's better for you to know things early and we begin planning early. You will need too many things to resume school and I have to begin looking for money early enough." Maria made supper and they ate together again. Jimmy would talk then all of a sudden keep quiet. Maria realised it.

"Why do you keep quiet like that?"

"I am planning."

That night they talked until late. Maria took the chance to tell Jimmy her mind.

"Maria, do you think you are going to pass your exams?"

"Yes, I have a strong belief. Things might fail me but my hope has not yet failed me."

"If you pass, how do you hope to live?"

"That's one big problem. Jimmy, I told you that I was not ready for a child and you made it on your own. What are you going to do about it? You told me you would handle it. Now is the time," Jimmy kept quiet. He had asked Maria that question expecting to get another answer. He didn't know it would lead him to a trap.

"We shall see to that, Maria."

"No, Jimmy let's discuss it now. I want to know what you are planning to do about it. It's all your problem. I told you I was not ready and you made it on your own."

111

"Maria, you are taking things for granted. It's as if you have known you have passed. What if you fail?"

"No, that's out. You tell me what you are going to do. You told me I should leave here because you have a wife. This is the right time to settle everything, then I leave you and your wife in peace."

"Are you quarrelling again? Are you bitter with me?"

"I am not quarrelling, I am not bitter, I am simply serious about what is at hand. Many a time, when I ask about how something will be handled, you tell me you will see. You later on deliberately forget and then when things get worse you to do it by mishandling me."

"Maria, you are still bitter about the incident that took place at the party. How many times do you want me to repeat? If you can't forget then I don't know what I should do!"

"I have long forgotten that. I am thinking about my future."

"If that is what is worrying you Maria, I will settle that. I know this world better than you do. I have had more problems than you have had. This one is no problem, we shall get through."

"Jimmy, I am tired of your house. I have been abused in all ways here under your roof and I want to get myself out of it. I never expected this of you, Jimmy. I don't want to live such a life again. I'd rather die. It's the right time for me get my freedom. You will not delay my freedom by suspending problems."

"Maria, the way you talk, when you get out of here, does it mean you will not want me?"

"No, I can't come back here to be starved, to be beaten, to have no company but worries, I cannot come here to be told to get out. No!"

"So you will not marry me?"

"No!"

"Why?"

"You told me you have your wife and you can't be a polygamist. Your wife told me to leave you alone, that you are my father not husband and I tell you that I can't marry you because you are not humane!"

"Maria, so that's what you have been harbouring in your heart?"

"Because of what you did to me!"

"So you don't want me?"

"No!"

"And you will not change your mind?"

"No! I want freedom, liberty. I want to rest from this for good! I am tired of this world, I am tired of suffering. I want to rest!"

"Please, Maria..."

"No." She coiled away from him. "I am not going to forgive you for all you have done to me. I curse, I curse, I pray to God to help me."

"I love you, Maria." She turned her face away and spat. Jimmy didn't see. It was dark. "Maria, I love you."

"You can give the love to someone else, I don't want it!" Jimmy laughed. It was a mocking laugh and he turned his face away. Maria didn't care. She was yearning for freedom and she longed for the morning. They fell asleep deep in their separate thoughts.

Maria woke up early in the morning. She opened the window and a cold breeze entered the room. Jimmy felt cold and he told her to shut it fast. She did as he said and went out. She sat on the verandah and started brushing her teeth in the open. When she got up to go she turned her eyes to the east. The sun was rising. It was beautiful and Maria could not tell what feelings it gave her. It was as if she was witnessing the sunrise for the first time. She caught herself shedding tears. I am a fool, she thought. What makes me behave so? She went in and started making breakfast. Jimmy got up and brushed his teeth. They took breakfast together but in silence, each having their own thoughts.

"This could be the last time I am having breakfast with you," Maria thought. Then she smiled. Inside her, she felt at peace, her heart was already free. It was now the body. "But I am stupid," she thought again, "After this we shall have to wait for some weeks before we get to the higher institutions. Probably Makerere or the diploma colleges."

"Well, but at least I have hope. Freedom is coming." She got excited. It would be fun getting together with her teachers today. She could even meet some classmates. She immediately stopped eating and started dressing. She was through. Jimmy gave her money and she was soon gone.

She sat quietly in the bus and looked out through the window. Fear started building up in her. She closed her eyes and tried to imagine what she had got but she failed. She wanted to get to school so fast and yet she feared to reach it. She went back to looking through the window again. She tried to crane her neck to see the distance ahead. Then a woman just in front of her pushed her head through the window and started vomiting. The vomit remained hanging in the air. She started feeling nausea. She tried to control it: the distance to school was now very short and she did not want to vomit there.

Immediately she got out of the bus, Maria started vomiting. She hung around the bus stage until she felt she was fine. However, she was still weak. Now she walked to the school. Her heart shrank but her legs drew her nearer, and the nearer she drew, the stronger the feeling of failure became and the more she wanted to run away. All the same, her legs took her. She entered the headmaster's office almost in stealth. Immediately he saw her, he got up and embraced her.

"Congratulations!" Then he shook her hand as if he was going to pluck her arm off her body. Maria sighed in relief. At least he had warmed her up. "Congratulations!" the headmaster said again, this time louder. "Thank you," Maria replied and added a smile to it.

The headmaster smiled back and resumed his seat, then showed Maria to a seat opposite his desk. He took some paper from a drawer and started showing them to Maria. He looked at her and smiled. Maria shed tears. He saw. "Excited?" he asked her.

"I can't believe it, sir."

"Yes, it's hard to believe, but it's the truth, Adirisa. You ought to laugh your head off. So, congratulations again and perhaps again and again." He laughed.

"Thank you, sir," Then she made to leave.

"Oh, why so early! Your teachers will want to see you and hug you. Your friends who are soon facing the battle you have gone through will want to ask for your prayers, I would want to honour you with a meal with me ... the list is long Adirisa. Don't you see?" He laughed again and Maria joined him this time. Inside her, she was eager to go before the teachers and students noticed her. Some of them were too keen and they would suspect her. What if they asked her a question such as "Are you not pregnant?" What would she say? What would be the reply?

"Thank you, sir, but I have to hurry away. I am sorry. I have to get back home and get some work done. You see, we have to help the parents search for money, otherwise we shall never see school again."

"No, Adirisa, you are only eager to break the news to your father and then hens will begin losing their heads. Yes, it's not easy to read and the parents have to be proud of such great success."

114

"So, I have to get going."

"Since you insist, I cannot hold you back." He got up and opened the door. Maria followed him from behind. "But it is bad you have refused my offer."

"No, sir, I am busy now but when I get time I will come back and have all the offers and ask for me. Obviously, I will have to come back here. I am an old girl now and I cannot forget my school."

"Yes, you have to come back. You have got to come back and encourage those other sisters of yours." The headmaster took her up to the school gate and said goodbye: "Greet your parents and tell them we share the happiness. Let him kill as many hens as possible." He laughed. "Goodbye, Adirisa. I wish you success still in a lot more. I hope I will see you as a great woman."

"Goodbye, sir." And she turned her back to him and left. He also went away immediately. She was happy no one else saw her apart from the secretary. She had fixed Maria with her eyes but after all she was alone and it would take time for her to convince the whole school. The headmaster was too excited. He seemed not to have noticed anything. She now prayed that she would not see any teachers or students on her way. Back at the bus stage Maria waited impatiently. The atmosphere was too tense for her. She kept on looking in all directions to assure herself that no one who knew her was around. At long last, the bus came.

The moment she entered it, she felt safe and she breathed heavily, ceremoniously, as if to say goodbye. She had escaped notice. She felt comfortable and an inner peace reigned in her. The feeling of the morning came back to her. This time it was as if she was seeking the world for the first time. She saw great beauty in the dull grass, in the bushy trees, in everything. She wanted to hold the whole world in her heart, she wanted to embrace it, to show it that she loved it. How it would be sweet to have her parents before her! She felt like crying, like laughing, like smiling and yet she frowned. It was as if she was bitter, as if there was some sweetness. She was excited and yet she caught in her a low spirit, almost dying. She got mixed up and she wanted to cry. But why was she having such a feeling? It must be out of her success. She had passed very well and it would be news to all who would hear. Perhaps the bitterness is because she will never have the chance to tell her father that she had gone through her exams. No that can't be the reason why. She had passed exams several times and it was no longer a miracle to her. Then she remembered she was about to get her freedom. She would be free from Jimmy, his wife and all. She would never worry, she would never be beaten or shouted at. She would be free, as free as a bird in the air. No more crying. Maria sighed, and she felt the weight of mixed feelings creep out of her heart. "What a feeling towards freedom! It's hard to wait at the gates of freedom," she said aloud and started thinking ahead.

She would go home and break the news to Jimmy. She had left Jimmy waiting. He was not going to go anywhere until Maria returned. Yesterday night he had refused to tell me what he was planning to do about me because he said I may not go through. He wanted to plan one way. He had refused to say in case you have failed, in case you have passed. Now today, the results were here, and she had passed! Yes, I will show him the results and demand to hear his plans. Of course I am not going to submit to marriage. That is no plan. I want to go back to school. Whatever he will choose to do. I just want to be free from this weight in my womb. Then when I am well it will be time to report for studies. He will send me to school and I swear by my own self, that will be the end of any relationship between me and Jimmy. I will be patient with my parents. The news of my breakthrough will obviously have to reach them in two days' time and who knows with this success, he might forgive me before I get back to school. It could be after sometime, could be after my first term. I don't care how long he will take, as long as we die reconciled.

Yes, I am happy there is living hope for me. I want to go and read and I will have my revenge. Jimmy must pay for my suffering. I may not do anything to him. He might be so desperate and will only deserve sympathy. All the same, I have to stand on my two feet, I will get back on track and show Jimmy that falling is not failing. I have to win him in one way or another. He will have to want me again and I will have to spit in his face. Very sweet revenge!

For now, I have to give up men for some time. Five years, even fifteen. I have had a lesson that will never get out of my life. I had never imagined I would ever lead such a hard life but it's funny how things can happen. Well, I am getting through it. It has been months but it feels like I have had it for eighty years. It's true, hardship can multiply time. Nonetheless I don't care about that. I am happy I am on the road to freedom. I will soon be free and all that will be in the past. It will only be at the back of my head ...

The bus stopped and Maria got out. She hurried away immediately. A smile was on her face and pride in her heart. How was she going to break the news to Jimmy? She started planning it.

I will wear a sad face, then he will feel happy that I have not managed and when he is still laughing I will tell him the truth. This will have to frustrate him very much.

Or I will enter jubilating, I will jump and shout: "Freedom is come"! He will feel jealous and march out. I will be the heroine, after a long stormy night.

Or else I will enter the house just like on any day and keep quiet. He will ask me questions and when I don't answer, he will begin pleading. After he has pleaded I will ask him in a rude tone: "Do you expect a whole me to fail?" He will look at me with eyes of respect. He will have to know that he has been playing with someone who is not all that cheap. He will realise I have more brain than him. Any way can do but at least I have to pinch him by it.

No, why should I tell him first? I will rush to the neighbour and send her to my mother, my mother will then tell my father. They come first, Jimmy is an outsider and it's only the devil that fixes him. She saw the roof of the house and her heart started beating. She was going to surprise Jimmy. She hurried towards it.

The door was halfway open. "Why had Jimmy left it so?" Maria asked herself. She pushed it wide and entered. Then all of a sudden she stopped, looked around. She proceeded to the bedroom, then rushed back to the sitting room and stepped outside suddenly. It was as if the house were on fire. She went round the house. Jimmy's car was nowhere to be seen. Where had he gone? Then she went back to the sitting room. There was nothing left in it apart from two cheap cups and a plate. Maria turned round and saw nothing more. She entered the bedroom again but there was only the bed without the mattress. It was the only thing in the room. Maria opened the window and peeped through it. There was no sign of Jimmy. She closed it and sat on the empty bed. She saw a paper folded under the bed and picked it up. It bore her name. She unfolded it hurriedly. Jimmy had obviously left it for her. Was he on safari and informing her of where to get him? Had his wife taken everything in his absence and he had followed her up? She decided to read it.

Dear Maria,
I am gone! And where I go to, you will never find me. I have left you that house and whatever remains there, you can begin with that. I have been kind enough not to leave you empty handed. I hope you appreciate it.

Yours Jimmy

At first, she did not understand the letter. She read it again and again until she could believe the message. What has Jimmy done to me? At the eleventh hour he decides to walk out on me! What has Jimmy done to me? What am I going to do now? She got up as if to walk away, then sat back. From a distance, something was asking her, "What are you going to do?" She got up again and started moving round the house. What am I going to do? Why did I let Jimmy go? Why didn't I kill him before today? So Jimmy refused to tell me what he had proposed to do about me because this is what he was going to do. She felt a sudden bitterness and she sat down on the floor and wept. The more she wept the more she felt bitter and frustrated. "What has Jimmy done? What am I going to do?" she kept on asking herself. Ahead of her, she saw an emptiness, a void world. She was hanging in the air and she had nowhere to land. No hands waited to protect her. Everyone had ignored her. "What am I going to do?" She felt a pain running all over her head. It was as if her eyes were going to fall out. She got up and covered her face with her hands. Then she uncovered her face again. She sighed, "What am I going to do?"

The voice started again. Maria looked round to find where the voice was coming from. Just on the bar above the window, she saw some white bottles. She climbed on the bed, took them down and started opening them. She had put them there one day when she was cleaning and since then they had been forgotten. One of the bottles had yellow powder, she didn't know what it was. Another had some metal things. They must have been Jimmy's. The other two contained tablets. Probably

118

aspirins but the other she didn't know. She got one aspirin and chewed it. It will help me with my headache. For a while, her thought ceased. The voice started haunting her again. What are you going to do? As if asking the voice, Maria said aloud," What am I going to do?" She cried for a long time. Then she kept quiet again and looked at the bottles. She stared at the aspirins. "They could also help," she said aloud and wiped her tears.

Her mind started wandering. Her thoughts were wild. "Jimmy wherever you are, let God's wrath find you. This is what you have led me to. You have led me to my doom. Oh, God forbid. You can't forbid. It's too late. God, what are you thinking in heaven above? Are these the things you sit on your throne planning? God, just picture yourself in my position, just picture yourself man as I am without any godliness, don't you think it would have been too much for you? Don't you think you would have taken a wild step? God, in your judgement don't be principled, look at things the way they happen. But I am too greedy. Sorry for being too greedy to whosoever is living in me. My mother made me see the rising and setting of the sun yet my greed is making me deprive you of it. Sorry! But you will have to understand me. It's better you remain where there is peace other than coming here to suffer like me. Do you get me?"

She waited for an answer but she got none. "Whatsoever you are thinking, I am doing this for both your good and mine. This world is bad, how can it treat me like this? How can it throw me away as if it has never mothered me? But I yearn to leave you. I hate you, as if I have never lived in you. I wish I had another world. Oh God, have mercy upon me. Pity me in my plight, God, don't be principled, don't be rigid but be fair in thy judgement, be pragmatic. Lord, I wish I could sit near you, I don't want to be in this world any more. I am going to remain here, I will remain here in Jimmy's house. I will stay here until they get concerned. Then they will come here and find me alone. They will ask for Jimmy and I will keep quiet. They will conclude that I don't know. Then they will begin searching for him, they will get him and ask him why he has left me alone. I will keep quiet and wait for his answer. Whether he wins or he loses, I will keep quiet. I will not talk, I am tired. God judge me and Jimmy but don't be principled. Let it be, let it be" Then louder she said "Let it be ...!"

She started swallowing the aspirins rapidly and soon the bottle was empty. She looked around, no one was watching, then she started crying violently. Jimmy why did you do that to me? My father why did you deny me? My mother why can't your energies work? Even the world has thrown me away. God, why can't you then take me? The world has rejected me. Where do you expect me to go? Mother, mother, mother, where are you? It's time to say goodbye! I-t i-s t-i-m-e to- s-a-y G-o-o-db-y-e.

She felt the world rolling round her, it rolled and rolled and rolled. Then bells started ringing, grasshoppers started chirping. She felt like vomiting. She opened her eyes, the roof was down and the floor was up. Fear crept into her heart, why was the world upside down? She closed her eyes again. Her hands started groping for something to cling to but she could not find anything. She folded them on her chest, they were cold. Her head was thick, it was as if a whole mountain was resting upon it. The bells around her increased. She was irritated and shouted at them to stop.

She opened her eyes to see who was creating the noise but she could not leave them open for a long time, the eyelids were too heavy. However, she was able to see the person ringing the bell. It was the time-keeper at school. It was prayer time and yet the students were still sleeping, so he kept on ringing to wake them up. Then all of a sudden, they were in the chapel. Maria could not tell how they had got there and yet, some few seconds ago, they had been in bed. The door to the chapel was closed and it remained dark and quiet. Maria was about to scream when the lights were turned on. The priest started leading the prayers. Then from nowhere he picked her to take the reading. She obeyed but her heart was beating with fear. It was going to be the first time she would take a reading. Was she going to stand before the congregation? She took heart. The priest did not even tell her where to get the reading from. She decided to open anyhow. It was the book of Revelations, chapter twenty one and verse four. It was exactly where the priest wanted.

She started reading and before she had gone halfway, the priest came and stopped her. She looked around the congregation in embarrassment. Then she saw her mother open the door to the chapel carefully and slip inside. Maria made to run to her but she found that her legs were in chains. She was so surprised. All along, she had not known that the legs of those who took readings were put in chains. Then the priest forced her head back to the book. She had never heard of any such book in the Bible. She could not even pronounce the book so she decided to begin straight away with the reading. It was Chapter one, from verse one to three. The reading was strange to her but she shouted it.

He comes on
Like a King, like a general
Riding on his mighty horse
With his mighty spear in his iron hand
Assured of his mighty strength
Depending on his unquestionable powers
Nothing will bar his way.

"Brothers and sisters, this is the word of God," Maria concluded but she received no reply from the congregation. She took a breath and looked up. There was no one in the chapel with her. It was dark, there was no window and the only door was locked with a heavy padlock. She looked back, even the priest had left sometime earlier. She started panicking. Some unpleasant noise started drumming round her ears. Then she head the hoofs of a horse cracking the ground. She held her breath, she saw the door of the chapel burst open. It was the conqueror, he was riding on his horse and he had come to conquer her, Maria. She tried to run away, she tried in all directions but it was too dark, she could not make any progress. He caught her and lifted her onto his horse.

They travelled to lands she did not know. It was frightening. They reached remote rocks and he left her there alone. Maria started groping for her way alone. She groped between rocks. It was very quiet and too chilly. She was frightened, she kept on looking round but she could not even see her nose. She felt like going back but something kept her going ahead. On she went ...

Maria lay on the ground, cold and motionless. Her mother sat next to her body, beat her breasts and cried," I wish it was yesterday, if it was yesterday or even some minutes earlier. It is too late." Outside the birds sang their last tunes before they went to sleep. The sun was setting to the west and, from the east, the moon was impatient. Everything went on like any other day but one thing was true, Adirisa was no more. She had gone through the window of life.